Last Ch[...]

When Dad left and I came home from school and journ[...] taped to the fridge I coped beautifully. The letter said he'd gone to St Kitts to live, that it was just something he had to do and sorry and look after the twins.

Julian's dad has run off to St Kitts, leaving him to look after his six-year-old twin sisters, with only a cash card and two Fuzzballs, the latest toy craze, to help him. Julian tries to cope on his own, but finds it hard to fit in his schoolwork and running practice as well, especially when the twins suddenly start behaving oddly. Julian is convinced it is the Fuzzballs that are causing the twins' erratic behaviour and tries to find out why—but no one else seems to have noticed anything. So Julian decides to stake everything on one last chance to prove he is right . . .

Patrick Cave was born in Bath, Somerset, and educated at Wells Cathedral School, St Martin's College (Lancaster), and the University of North Wales. He has taught English in various parts of Britain and Greece, and currently lives in France, having moved to work at Bordeaux University. He believes that children's fiction is the purest and most honest form of telling the stories of our existence. 'It's a pity,' he says, 'that when we grow up we often learn to paint life pictures with very drab and limited horizons and then find that we have to live there ourselves.' When he is not writing he enjoys cross-country running, tennis and skiing, as well as music and 'green causes'. *Last Chance* is his second novel for Oxford University Press.

Last Chance

Other novels by Patrick Cave

Number 99

'A very readable novel . . . The theme is developed without moralizing or sentimentality . . . '
The Guardian

'A thriller-ish pace dense with plans, counter-plans, and chases . . . a strong first novel . . . '
The Times Educational Supplement

'a thriller tied up with GM crops, a story of greed and dishonesty and a story of strong relationships. I loved it and had to read it all in one sitting . . . '
Literacy and Learning

'Compelling . . . this book is a great and engaging read. Kez is a particularly memorable and strong character.'
Abby Ajayi, Children's BBC

'I enjoyed it . . . [A] good mix of contemporary issues and the personal . . . '
Francine Stock, writer and broadcaster

Last Chance

Patrick Cave

OXFORD
UNIVERSITY PRESS

OXFORD
UNIVERSITY PRESS

Great Clarendon Street, Oxford OX2 6DP

Oxford University Press is a department of the University of Oxford.
It furthers the University's objective of excellence in research, scholarship,
and education by publishing worldwide in

Oxford New York

Auckland Bangkok Buenos Aires
Cape Town Chennai Dar es Salaam Delhi Hong Kong Istanbul
Karachi Kolkata Kuala Lumpur Madrid Melbourne Mexico City Mumbai
Nairobi São Paulo Shanghai Taipei Tokyo Toronto

Oxford is a registered trade mark of Oxford University Press
in the UK and in certain other countries

British Library Cataloguing in Publication Data available

ISBN 0 19 275241 3

1 3 5 7 9 10 8 6 4 2

Typeset by AFS Image Setters Ltd, Glasgow

Printed in Great Britain by
Cox & Wyman Ltd, Reading, Berkshire

To Loïc, for being brave and loving

1

A psychiatrist is someone who helps you if you're mentally ill. If you just have difficulty coping with normal life you can see a psychologist. That's what *my* psychologist told me one day when I asked the difference out of boredom.

But then I didn't have any difficulty coping with anything.

When Dad left and I came home from school and found his letter taped to the fridge I coped beautifully. The letter said he'd gone to St Kitts to live, that it was just something he had to do and sorry and look after the twins.

I stood there and read it and didn't feel much of anything.

I coped.

Oh yeah, I knew that *he* needed a psychiatrist—that you didn't just walk out one morning and emigrate and leave three children when the other parent had already left years before. Most people would think that doing that was more than just not coping.

Final proof of the madness was what he'd left us to survive. A cashpoint card that he said in a PS would be good for about £3000 until we put more in, a plastic bag with some present or other for the twins, and instructions for his flaming betting system.

I opened the bag and found what our loving dad had got his girls.

Fuzzballs.

Two shiny boxes and, inside, furry beasts with demonic eyes and little jutting teeth, and pink, heart-shaped labels tied round their necks saying that they were both called Karko.

Bloody hell, Dad, I thought, don't you know the twins never want things to be the same? I'd already seen great stacks of the Fuzzball monsters in the shops, all different colours and shapes, ready to be doled out at Christmas, and Dad couldn't even find two different ones.

That was mainly what I thought, standing with the letter in one hand and the Fuzzball bag in the other, looking out on the bright green turf Dad had poisoned the garden with. Also, that the fridge noise was too loud. About him leaving, well, like I said, I didn't feel much of anything about that.

Coping was so easy. That psychologist must be mad.

When I'd looked out on the same garden six years ago—when I was almost nine—it was much bigger and half wild. There was a little silvery tree in the middle with coloured, trailing things Mum had made hanging from it, and sprawling bushes and bright peeping flowers, and all of Mum's statues. Great heavy chunks of honeyed stone—oolite, Mum said—that came on a truck in uneven lumps, got dumped down on the grass right next to where Dad drove up the back lane and parked his Escort . . . and then got tapped and felt and cut and teased into flowing, puzzling, or abrupt new shapes before reluctant Dad had to ask the neighbours to help him wrestle and drag the finished thing to whatever spot Mum felt was right.

The grass at the end was always white with stone dust, and Mum was out in all weathers working her stone, whiter even than the dust.

One of her statues stood next to the back door looking out and up towards the top of the silver tree and the sky beyond. It was called Self and was beautiful and slender like Mum and had her long hair and all, but was quite frightening too because the arms and legs and parts of the face were rearranged and not where they should be, like a Picasso painting. Mum told me that it was her best work. Dad hated it so much that when she left he went to the garage on the corner and borrowed a crowbar and a lump hammer and very calmly knocked it to pieces.

I can still see the pile of scarred stone body parts that were left when he finished.

Aged almost-nine, I thought he'd done it because the statue was naked and was supposed to be Mum.

At five-twenty the twins tumbled in from Mrs Sykes's car, laughing and jostling to get the best TV spot and called out, 'Beep-beep, *Ju*-lian. Beep-beep, *Jules*. Beep-beep, *Da*-ddy.'

I walked in to the lounge and said, 'Beep-beep, Tophie. Beep-beep, Sanya,' and they giggled at my serious face and shushed me to let them hear the TV and asked for Coke.

I got them juice, one in a wine glass, one in a pint mug, and decided to let them watch and not to tell them about Dad yet. Instead I sat at the little table in the corner and pretended to do homework while I watched my sisters' faces and wondered how long £3000 would last.

Sophie and Tanya nudged and giggled and sometimes fought or tumbled across the sofa onto the carpet in front of the telly, never needing to speak, never still, almost always grinning. When the wine glass got kicked over they both froze and became identically serious, holding their breaths and looking up at me, and then dissolved back into spluttering giggles as I went to get a cloth and wasn't angry.

'Sorry, *Ju*-lian. Beep. We're sorry.'

The twins had been born a few months before Self got crowbarred, but not to my mum. They came from Dad and one of his maths students at the college, a Nigerian girl who was pleased to have them and then fly back home. That made them the blackest of us, rich and dark and healthy, then Dad, then me, then my mum, who was white.

For tea I did pizzas. There were pre-done bases in the freezer that just needed spreading over with tomato paste and then bits of whatever you fancied stuck on top. The twins' programme finished and they bustled in to help and confidently glued banana chunks, mushrooms, single baked beans, and peanuts on to the tomato of their pizzas, looking disgusted at my bright peppers and olives and squealing in protest when I stopped them putting chocolate too; but then Sophie suddenly said, 'Where's Daddy?' and Tanya echoed, 'Yeah, *Ju*-lian, where's *Da*-ddy? Beep?'

'Oh, yeah: Daddy's gone away for a little bit. Not too long, I expect. He left some presents, look!'

Well, that lie worked until bed.

They ripped open the bag, of course, yelling, '*Fuzzballs*, yeah, Fuzzballs, *yeah*, cool!' when they saw the first corner of the boxes. Then when they both held a box and realized the creatures were the same one, they just stopped dead like they sometimes did, and looked at each other, then

4

each took out their Karko and solemnly gave it to the other.

'Cool,' I heard one of them whisper as they took the twin Karkos upstairs to be put in their beds.

After the pizzas, when I'd bullied them through the teeth and pyjama thing and had my hand on the lightswitch, Sophie asked again, 'Where's Daddy?'

'Gone,' I said. 'For a few days anyway.'

I flicked the light off and said goodnight and knew that my half-sisters were going to miss Dad a lot more than I was.

Me, well, I didn't feel a thing except that Dad should've been here to tell his daughters just why he had to go to bloody St Kitts and leave them.

Most of the evening I just felt bored. I wanted to run. In the end I took the paper about the betting system and read and thought about that until bed.

2

Usually when I called up in the mornings the twins fell down the stairs and went instantly to full power, which was how they seemed to live all their waking lives.

The next morning I called and nothing happened, so I went up.

'Come on. Mrs Sykes'll be here in twenty minutes . . . '

One little corner of curtain had been dragged back and Tanya stood swaying sleepily on one leg trying to get a sock on. Sophie was still in bed, cuddling her Karko, just watching her sister and humming quietly.

It wasn't what they did.

'Beep?' I said. 'Mrs Sykes? School? Beep-beep-beep. Earth calling.'

Tanya sat down suddenly on the floor to try the sock there and said, 'No beeping today, *Ju*-lian. It's Thursday.'

Actually it was Wednesday, but I stopped beeping and asked Sophie, 'Are you ill?'

'No. Find some clothes, please, Jules?'

'I have to get ready too.' But I found some clothes for Sophie and then some for Tanya and neither of them made a fuss at my choice or tried to wear wellies or slippers or leotards.

I thought that I would take them to the doctor if they seemed bad after school.

In the end I just managed to push them out of the door, clutching cereal bars for breakfast and bananas for tea, in time for Mrs Sykes's horn.

No beeping today, Mrs Sykes, I thought, waving to her. Today's Wednesday. Mrs Sykes was OK, though I thought she mainly bothered with us because there was only one black family in this bit of town and she wanted some sort of mission.

As she pulled away, the best of our mostly-dodgy neighbours—Mr Hermes over the road—appeared at his front door, so I kept the hand in the air, waving. He looked vaguely round, up and down the street, then saw me and slowly held his own hand up too. I thought he must be going to work, but when the waving finished he went back inside.

I hoped he was OK, not losing it or anything. Old Hermes had always been kind. To Mum, to me, now to the twins. All of us had sat in his kitchen one time or another, spooning down *kataifi*, which was Greek pastry or something swimming in syrupy sugar and nuts.

He never seemed to run out of foil trays of *kataifi*.

Where I could I'd chosen all sciences for my GCSE subjects, but of course I still had to do lessons like English Literature and a 'self-development' thing that everyone did, although not for an exam, just to learn about drugs and sex and how society worked.

I didn't worry about very much but I did worry a little that I might be just like Dad.

7

The sciences, especially maths, were all easy for me, even if I couldn't see the point. We sat there and shunted numbers or chemical symbols backwards and forwards like pushing little groups of dried beans around a table top . . . and as my beans usually got to their destination first the teachers were pleased. It kept your brain busy, but last year's maths guy had said happily that equations were like the music of Bach and that seemed nuts to me with those dead numbers.

Music's supposed to make you cry or leap about or at least tap your foot, isn't it? Even I know that.

Like Dad, the numbers were easy for me and the other things were impossible and without any sense. Last year's maths guy left with a breakdown, anyway.

That morning it was English. Shakespeare. Some famous bit, Mrs Lamb said, about the different ages of people and what they were like at each age.

It started by saying that life was like being actors in a play. 'All the world's a stage.' I didn't ask Mrs Lamb if you were acting when you were a baby and crying because you wanted milk, or if you were acting when you got run over or needed a hip replacement or had to do English Literature on Wednesdays. That kind of thing made her angry even if you really wanted the answers, which I didn't.

At least the shunted beans in maths weren't trying to be anything more special.

When we'd read the speech and talked about it, we had to write something like it in our own words, about people now in their different parts of life. I wrote about someone in China growing rice, with just three ages instead of the seven in the Shakespeare speech: being a baby, working all day to grow rice, and then being too old to grow rice and waiting to die.

Mrs Lamb said over my shoulder, 'Julian, why do you

deliberately try to do something which isn't the thing I asked for?'

Did I do that? It didn't feel like I was trying to make trouble.

I sometimes thought about how calm Dad had been when he was swinging that crowbar.

Wednesday afternoons was sport. The best thing we did. Since the minibus wasn't there to take us to the greenbelt urban park—a litter-filled mini valley running past the old car assembly plant and the new PVC factory—we did training laps round the edge of the school field, next to the blue, peeling gas containers. Walk one side, jog two, then sprint the last. Then do it again, and again, ten times.

I did twelve laps with a three second difference between the first and last, and thought about Dad's betting system.

Actually, he'd written down more than one system.

Start with the first one, he'd scrawled, *an idiot could make that one work, even if it doesn't make much profit. Small bets, boy, to start with. Don't bet just on one sport. Don't get interested in the sport you bet on.*

Fat chance.

Call your Aunt June when the money goes.

That last bit settled it. The dose I'd had of Aunt June six years ago had been too much already. The £3000 and the betting system—or a job maybe—would have to do.

'Park Grange on Saturday, Julian. Two o'clock.'

'OK, Mr Hewlett.'

Wondering what I'd do with the twins at two o'clock on Saturday, I cut off through the corner gate and along the smokers' lane onto the main road. A gang of idiots at a bus stop shouted in my face and one stuck out a foot to try and trip me. Liz was calm and friendly like every time. Not the same sort of calm as Dad's: a more worrying sort.

Liz is my psy-*cholog*-ist by the way.

We sat down, me on the sofa, her sitting very perfectly on a hard chair with a bowl of tea, and after about five minutes she said, 'So, tell me what's been happening in your life?'

Dad's gone west and unless I can make his betting system work I won't be able to pay a psychologist, Liz.

I told her about the Shakespeare and Mrs Lamb as I knew that was the sort of stuff she liked. She listened calmly and nodded. 'Why did you choose someone in China, Julian?'

'I don't know.'

'Do you know a lot about people living in China? Is it something you're interested in?'

'Not really, no. I just imagined it.' The sweat from my twelve laps and then running here was cool now. I needed my shower.

'Imagination is good. We all need that. Maybe in China there's a boy imagining the different stages of *your* life for his teacher, Julian.'

I didn't think there was, but I knew what was next.

'What do you think he might imagine? Doing it like the Shakespeare.'

Without wanting to I did think about that. What would he say about the stage of life I was in right now? For a moment my life seemed so different from anything I'd ever known, so flaming *unlikely* . . .

'That boy'd have to be a bloody genius, Liz.'

She put her tea bowl down and smiled at me.

'How are the twins?'

Like usual she zeroed gently in on things she thought we ought to talk about and then see-sawed back to everyday stuff for a while. Twenty-five minutes today, which meant she thought the session had been 'useful'. (If it went to forty, we'd wasted our time).

'You ought to ask for Mrs Lamb's job, Liz.'

'You know, I might just do that.'

She was very different to me and sometimes irritated me with her games, but it was hard not to like her.

Running back, the same idiots were at the same bus stop and we went through the same shout-and-trip routine as before. Either the buses were doing really badly today or that stop was some kind of meeting place. An advert across the street caught my eye as I dodged the waiting foot:

FUZZBALLS ARE HERE!

Next year it would be some other fool craze, but the bus-stop gang would probably still be there, waiting to evolve.

One of the things Dad lost because of that thing with the Nigerian girl—the twins' mum—was his job as maths lecturer at the college. Since then he'd supported us mostly by betting.

Any betting system works on probabilities. There'll be a certain number of times that you lose so you need to have enough cash to cover that, but if you can guess or work out roughly how often you might win, you can work out a system that *should* make money.

That's the theory anyway.

Dad's System No.1—that 'an idiot could make work' (thanks, Dad)—worked by you just placing bets when the odds were 2 to 1. That means that the people who take your bet think that the racing car or dog or whatever has a good chance of winning (about 33 per cent) and if it or he does win they'll just pay back double your money, plus your stake.

The idea was to start with a small bet, and each time you lost, to double the size of the bet next time, *plus* the

11

difference between the two previous bets. It didn't say if there was a difference to add for bet number 2, when there hadn't been two previous bets yet. If there *wasn't* and you started with a bet of £1, I worked out the progression should be: £1, £2, £5, £13 . . .

If that all sounds mental, ask your maths teacher.

Running home I saw a betting shop and without thinking about it just went in. It wasn't a modern chain, just a dingy one-off place with a blank window, 'E. George and Sons, Bookmakers'. I had one pound and put it on a horse called Pine Nut who was apparently in the last race that day at Exeter.

'Are you eighteen?' The old bloke on the other side of the glass looked about a hundred and eighteen and was half hidden by smoke from the fag hanging on his lip.

'No, nineteen.'

At the house Mrs Sykes's car was already sitting outside.

'All right, Julian, love? I was a bit worried, with nobody in. Your dad not there?'

'No, he'll be back later.'

Much much later.

'Well . . . OK then.' She looked doubtful and I thought about hot water and clean clothes. 'If you need me, you know where I am.'

'Yes. Thank you.'

The twins raced up the path, hopping, and fell over giggling together in front of the door. Tanya screwed up her face and said very slowly, 'Us . . . already . . . asked . . . she.'

Sophie nodded seriously. 'Dad . . . about.'

'Oh, God,' I said, catching on. 'Can't we beep again instead?'

They looked at each other, stood up, and said together: '*Ju*-lian . . . no.'

We went in and I spent a long time in that shower.

When I came out, the twins were hugging their Karko Fuzzballs, watching a programme about sheep farming. When I flicked over for five minutes to see Pine Nut win his race easily ('KO, girls . . . moment . . . a . . . for . . . just?') they didn't bother to complain.

3

Like Pine Nut, I had no problems winning against Park Grange on Saturday. I wondered if he'd had the same sense of peace that I got from being out alone in front.

Mr Hewlett said happily, afterwards, 'Like a machine, eh, Julian?'

Park Grange were pretty rubbishy, but the truth was that I only knew how to run one kind of race. From the gun I just had to be in front, with clear distance between me and the next idiot. It was one of the only strong feelings I had.

'What about that f**king pain, man, going up that first hill? Don't you *feel* that?' Curtis Anderson asked me, in disgust . . . and the answer was honestly no, though I didn't tell him that. When I was at the front with just clear ground ahead—even if the ground went up—and with only my heartbeat and breathing and the smell of the air going up a hundred miles, I just didn't feel a thing. Only peace.

What kind of machine was that?

Mrs Sykes had been sorted out by me forging a letter from Dad.

Dear Mrs Sykes,

Thank you so much for your continuing kindness in ferrying my daughters backwards and forwards from school.

I wonder if you would also possibly be able to look after them for a couple of hours this Saturday afternoon? I am very busy at the moment with training for a new job as commercial representative, and Julian will unfortunately be racing on Saturday while I am away, though he will be able to call for them by four-thirty.

Sorry that this is such short notice.

Yours
Don Egg

It sounded right to me, but I thought that if it wasn't Mrs Sykes would put it down to Dad being black, even though he'd been a college lecturer. The lie was so easy, like the race.

I sat on a bench outside the shopping centre until almost four-thirty thinking about nothing much, then jogged to where Mrs Sykes lived. Hayley answered the door, wearing lots of make-up and blushing.

'Hi, Julian. Did you win? Do you want a drink?'

Hayley was at my school, in the class below mine. I never knew what to say to her.

'Hi. Yes . . . and no drink, thanks.'

'Mum!' she called. 'Julian's here! He won again!'

Mrs Sykes came in and asked me again if I wanted a

drink, and made me eat some cake, and said how happy she was that Dad had found a job.

'It must be so difficult,' she said. 'Do tell him he can rely on me to help with the twins.'

I didn't ask what it was that must be so difficult. I thanked her for Dad, and then she (deliberately?) left me with Hayley, who talked about what music she liked in the charts and asked if I ever went out to the cinema or anything like that. When the twins burst in with their coats and bits of cake wrapped up to take home, I think Hayley was as relieved as me, though she still stuck around and watched me through the hall and out of the door.

'See you at school, Julian.'

I put one twin on each side, holding their hands, and went off down the street.

What's *wrong* with people? I thought, but maybe said it out loud, because Sophie, giggling, said, 'Hayley likes you, *Ju*-lian', and Tanya chanted, 'Likes you, likes you, likes you.'

'We'll bake some potatoes tonight,' I said, 'so you two horrors can help me choose something to put inside when we get home.' There wasn't one reason on earth why Hayley should like me.

Sophie chose tuna and Tanya wanted ice cream, but I lost them to their Fuzzballs when they'd made their choice. There were gum cards out now, which the twins had bought with the pocket money I got out of the machine that morning: pictures of the flaming things and (on the back) descriptions of their 'special powers'. The display in the shop said there were ninety-nine different Fuzzballs. Ninety-nine and we had two Karkos.

For the first time since Wednesday, the twins asked that night about Dad. Lying in bed, Sophie said, 'Dad's getting a new job . . . Mrs Sykes said.'

Tanya echoed dopily, 'New job . . . new job . . . new . . . when's he coming back?'

I'd expected them to ask again, and said that he would still be gone some time.

'We mustn't let Mrs Sykes know that, though. Or we'll have to have Aunt June to come and stay to look after us, until he gets here.'

They'd never met Aunt June, but the idea of someone new in the house was enough. '*You* look after us, *Ju*-lian. That lady don' know about ice cream on potatoes an' stuff.'

'No, I expect she doesn't know that.'

Dad had come back out to the garden while I was looking at the broken body parts from Self. It had started to rain, I remember, little darker circles appearing on the honey of the stone.

'Come on, boy, there's nothing to see there. The thing was all wrong anyhow.'

He was calm and in control and had triumphed with his tools over Self. He took my arm and pulled me to the car, standing next to the dust-filled, flattened grass down the back. We got in and drove away from there, hours and hours with the wipers squeaking and Dad's mathematic calmness filling the car.

'You're going to stay with your Aunt June for a while. You need a change.'

I'd have rather sat in Mr Hermes's kitchen, eating *kataifi*.

Then we arrived at a house I'd never seen before and he left me with a woman I'd never met before. Aunt June.

When Dad got me again, six months later, and drove me back, there was no stone dust, no tree, no Self. There was a gravel car space the right size for his car and shiny grass. Everything Mum had touched was gone and the twins, who were babies, had come to live with us.

Aunt June had spent the whole six months criticizing and sympathizing with Dad and pouring drink into her teacup and pulling at my hair with a comb and marching me to the school I went to at that time to try and make me point out who was bullying me, which I never would. I asked her if she liked Mum and she said sharply, 'Your father should've known better. That's all, boy.'

She was Dad's older sister and knew best about everything.

After Pine Nut I lost five bets in a row. For the last bet I watched the whole thing on TV, live from Chepstow. My horse was called Stinker and even when they were getting lined up for the start his head was down and he didn't seem to care. The horse that went on to win was black and giving little jumps and walking sideways. Even I could see that Stinker didn't want to be there that day.

Despite Dad's instructions all my bets were on horse races. I don't know why. Football seemed too complicated, about who would score first in which match, and there were no Formula One races or anything.

Also that week there was washing to do and a load of bills and visiting the giant Asda with the twins, coming back by minicab. Dad's card went in and out of the machine and the printed balance was now only £2739.

On Wednesday afternoon I did fifteen laps with just a two second difference and then threw up before jogging to my session with Liz.

'You look terrible,' she said, sipping her bowl of tea. 'Is there something special you'd like to talk about this week?'

Yes, Liz. Is there anything useful running in the four-thirty this afternoon?

'Mr Hewlett thinks I'm a machine, winning every race. One of my sisters was in trouble at school yesterday for throwing something at some kid. But the twins never fight. Not really.'

My insides squirmed. Don't give too much, or the sessions get heavy and complicated. No help to anyone.

'I see . . . is there a connection between these things at all? The races and the twins fighting, I mean. Why did you mention them together?'

'I don't know. You're the flaming expert.'

Liz grinned, never minding my rudeness.

'Do you *feel* like a machine? Our bodies are, of course, a bit like very special machines; but what do you think about or feel when you race?'

'I feel like a machine. One that can only work in that clear space at the front.'

'Do you have anything special in your head, out there at the front?' Liz was looking into her teabowl for the question and then looked up at me to see my answer. I wondered if she'd learnt that at psychologist school. Today was one of the times I found her games irritating.

'No.'

A pause.

'How's life at home? How are the twins? Apart from getting into trouble yesterday?'

'Everything's fine. The twins are mad anyway. Runs in the family. And it was them that told me—us—that they'd been naughty. No big deal.'

What was wrong with her? You couldn't expect them to be flaming angels twenty-four hours a day at their age. Maybe I should stop coming to see Liz. There was too much happening in my day. It didn't do any good, anyway. It was just for her, mostly.

I said, 'I have to go now.'

I didn't want nosy Mrs Sykes having time to ring the bell or anything while she was dropping the twins off, but jogging home I still drew out a wodge of Dad's money—our money—and stopped off at the betting shop.

'How old are you?' The same yellowed old man in his smoke.

'You always ask me. I'm nineteen.'

He gave a crackly sort-of-a wheeze, which might have been a laugh.

'Date of birth, Sonny Jim?'

I put my real birthday back by five years and he looked disappointed.

'What star sign is that, then?' he tried.

'Scorpio.'

At last he took my bet, muttering. Why didn't the fool ask for ID?

Mrs Sykes arrived at our house at the same time as me. She said brightly, 'Your father selling lots of . . . er . . . ?' She beamed at me, waiting to have the gap filled.

'Portable electronic organizers, Mrs Sykes. No. He's still training. There's a lot to learn, he says. They fit in the palm of your hand.'

Should I tell Liz how easy I found it to lie?

Over the road Mr Hermes was arriving in his Rover. Mr Hermes really *was* a rep, which was where I'd got the idea. Again I raised my hand to him as he looked over, but he didn't do anything this time except turn round and walk up his steps, stumbling a bit on the top one. I wondered if he was drunk.

The twins were almost hysterical that night, arguing about who had which halves of the orange pyjamas and the pink ones. I hardly recognized them, screaming at each other. They even threw their Fuzzballs.

After I'd washed up, I spent a long time just sitting in

the cold on the back step, wondering if I was giving them the wrong food. Perhaps they were missing Dad. Maybe it was too much TV, irradiating them.

I thought about Mrs Sykes and Liz. I thought about Aunt June and social services.

Even in the moonlight the lawn was shiny.

4

A month or perhaps two weeks back I hadn't known that Fuzzballs existed, but suddenly you didn't seem able to get away from them. (As usual) I wasn't sure if it was the world that was mad, or me. Shops were putting all their Fuzzball merchandise in special secure sections to avoid fights and shoplifting by parents desperate to get the creatures for Christmas presents. Schools had banned any Fuzzball stuff ever to be brought onto the premises. In Japan two children had actually died in some Fuzzball-related thing.

In the middle of it all, the Fuzzball creator, some American called Walter 'Lucky' Ferrin, decided to visit England. His stupidly long dark-red car, specially flown over from the States, appeared on all the news programmes. There were only the most shadowy shots of the guy himself, though, three-quarters hidden by the smoky car windows.

A huge, unsmiling, suit-wearing man with a ponytail and bulging forehead said on behalf of 'Lucky' Ferrin what a huge pleasure Lucky found it to be in good ol' England and how he'd like to make it a second home.

'Mr Ferrin intends to see *everything* on his trip to your island.'

It sounded more like a threat than a pleasure, from that monster.

At school I went on pushing the dried beans round and didn't get picked on too much by Mrs Lamb, although because Hallowe'en was coming up at the weekend she had us doing the three witches from flaming *Macbeth* and I had to read one of the parts out loud, which I avoided when I could.

> *Weary sennights nine times nine,*
> *Shall he dwindle, peak, and pine:*
> *Though his bark cannot be lost,*
> *Yet it shall be tempest-toss'd.*

What it meant I doubt anybody knew. People sniggered and Mrs Lamb stopped me after a few lines. 'That's fine, Julian, but can you be more of a squeaky, witchy old crone for us?'

I know that it was supposed to be fun for us, a break from usual lessons.

The same day, Hayley Sykes cornered me coming out of lunch. She looked miserable and white. I knew the signs. Here we bloody go, I thought.

Without any hello or anything she said, 'What are you doing for Hallowe'en?'

I almost lied again, then I relented and said, 'Nothing. Making costumes with the twins. Taking them round a couple of streets when it gets dark.'

She said something in almost a whisper. I hoped she wasn't going to faint.

'Sorry?'

'I said . . . may I come . . . and help . . . if your dad doesn't mind or anything. And there's a film . . . '

'OK,' I interrupted, 'come in the afternoon if you want.'

Weary sennights, nine times nine, I thought, that's what I feel like I've had. Hayley had already scooted off, but I felt so tired I almost couldn't stand up. Maybe none of us were eating right. Maybe too many cleaning products were soaking through my skin. Too many washing-up bubbles. Get it together, idiot.

I got my stuff and walked out of the school and to my home, where I lay on the sofa and watched horses all afternoon. Machines with glossy coats and large hearts bred to be in that front space with all the air above.

I'd have to try to be more like them.

Dad being in St Kitts, sitting sweating in the sun probably while our days were grey with mist and drizzle, didn't change the house one bit. We had clean clothes, hot food, enough toothpaste, and regular baths. If I'd had an address for Dad I'd have written and told him that.

I thought the twins might miss getting swept onto his lap once every couple of weeks to be told they were his special girls, allowed occasionally to poke and pull his face into funny shapes. If you knew my dad you'd know that was a treat. But in fact Sophie and Tanya calmed down again for a while and stopped even asking about Dad. I was still worried about them because looking after six-year-old girls wasn't easy and exact like balancing an equation or something, but we were doing OK. We hopped and beeped and stood on our heads.

More than coping.

My sixth bet in a row (£89!) had lost like the five before. The next one was due to be £233 and I'd already picked out a 2 to 1 horse called No Machine to back. On Saturday morning, though, the cashpoint would only give me £200, so I just went back home with the money to wait until Monday. That was the system.

For lunch I grilled some plantains while the twins sat at the kitchen table surrounded by this week's pocket-money Fuzzball stuff. Stickers and cards and Fuzzball comics, with free, 'amazing' Fuzzball combs.

It was good for my cooking that they were sitting down. This was a walking backwards day.

'Sophie! Plantain with . . . ?'

'*Choc*-olate, *Ju*-lian.'

'Please.'

'Please.'

'Tanya! Plantain with . . . ?'

'Spiders an' honey!'

'Please.'

'Spiders an' honey, please, *Ju*-lian.'

After some looking I managed to find an old packet of liquorice and started making it into spider shapes to sit on the plantain. Then the doorbell went and Hayley had come, even though it was still just one o'clock, so I asked her to do the spiders while I melted some chocolate.

Hayley was back to being pink again, not the white from before. I wondered just what we were going to do until trick-or-treating when it got dark. I wished there was a race again this week. Something for me.

'Your garden's a bit empty. Sad,' Hayley said, putting a giant tarantula carefully onto a slice of plantain.

Her smell was not what the kitchen was used to. Much too flowery for our house. Pink and white, like her.

I said, 'Dad likes it like that so there's not much work.'

'Oh.'

One thing that did surprise me was how good Hayley was with the twins. She took them up after lunch to wash, walking backwards with them, and when the three of them

25

got down again, the twins had somehow been persuaded to leave any trace of Fuzzballs upstairs and were going on about what they wanted to look like for trick-or-treating.

I sorted out anything I could find for dressing up and felt relieved knowing that it was really the twins Hayley had wanted to come and see.

While they got on with costumes in the kitchen I went to the sitting-room and watched No Machine cross the finishing line so far in front that no other horses were in the camera view at that moment. No Machine was still almost dancing as they took him to the 'Winner's Enclosure', which was a special little ring for everyone to congratulate each other and take their prizes. He seemed to know that he'd won and looked very pleased with himself.

The race after that had a very close finish, but a skinny brown horse (the announcer said it was 'chestnut') with a white nose was given it by the officials. His odds were ten to one. I'd have won £2330 pounds if I'd been able to get the money out and known to choose him. He knew that, grinning at the camera.

I watched maybe two more races—great dark chunks of earth getting thrown up by the horses' hooves as they slithered round in increasing rain, the jockeys clinging on with their bright colours sticking to their skin—and then someone said softly, 'They're beautiful, aren't they?'

Hayley was standing next to me. I realized I was still standing myself, my thumb resting on the remote control button that I'd pressed to turn the telly on.

I was almost angry that she was there and I hadn't known. I didn't usually get angry.

'Do you feel like that . . . when you race?'

That same flaming question. How do you feel when you race? How do you feel when you don't race? How do you feel when you pick your nose? As if it changed anything. My imaginary people in China would ask: *How*

much rice have you grown? She was still looking at the
screen, so that I saw her too-thin-and-pale face from the
side; and the question was just breathed. I couldn't really
be angry. Hayley was OK.

'I don't feel anything when I race.'

She looked at me and seemed puzzled. Then she sighed
and said, 'The twins are all done, very horrible, come and
see. Also . . . well, they're doing a special Hallowe'en
showing of the Fuzzballs movie this afternoon. I can treat
us if you like. I got my paper round money today. And
kids under ten get in free if they're in spooky costume.'

'The Fuzzballs *movie*?! There's a film now, too?' I
couldn't believe it. Just how did they produce this stuff so
quickly? Lucky Ferrin, that shadow in the dark red car,
seemed to have the whole flaming island going crazy.

'Julian!' Hayley was laughing at me. 'Of course there's
a film!'

Of course there was a film. Silly me.

I went and looked at the twins. Sophie was an alien,
green and silver with a washing-up bottle raygun. Tanya
was the walking dead, dripping in blood.

I said, 'You're not walking backwards when we go
out, too, are you?'

'Course,' Tanya said, and made a face at me to show
off her bloody fangs.

Somehow we made it to a bus stop and on into town.
The day at 3.15 was dim enough to be night.

When we got to the cinema we had to queue, standing
(backwards) in a mass of dressed-up kids, ghosts, witches,
and Frankensteins, some of them clutching Fuzzballs
brought from home. I hadn't let the twins bring theirs, in
case we were mugged for them. Forget mobile phones.

At the door we got Fuzzball badges and even tiny

27

mini-Fuzzballs themselves, just as ugly as the big ones. Mine was squat and grey like a pebble and 'called' Rockolo. Hours of thought had gone into that name.

'Do you want this?' I asked Hayley as we jostled up the stairs with the general tide. She shook her head, so I dumped my mini-Fuzzball into a bin, then added the badge too. After a moment Hayley did the same, which surprised me. Did she want to do it because I had? To impress me?

The cinema was huge and old-fashioned with blood-red, wooden-framed seats and a decorated and moulded cream-and-gold ceiling hung with chandelier things: not like the smart multiplex near the shopping centre. Every seat seemed to be full. A great sea of kids chewing and arguing and cuddling mini-Fuzzballs or the larger versions.

Did Hayley expect me to kiss her or something, when the lights went down? Why on earth had she chosen to spend her Saturday like this?

As they rolled the ads I felt restless, uncomfortable. We were in the middle of a row near the back. My head had started to ache. I wondered what would happen if I needed to go outside, to scream maybe. I thought deliberately of No Machine with his hard muscle and steaming breath and started to watch the story.

Apparently Fuzzballs were a gift from some aliens or some sort of unearthly power. Their 'seeds' or eggs or whatever had been left on our world long ago, to hatch out when they were really needed. Now they had awoken to help humans fight some massive threat. I wasn't sure what the threat was.

On all sides of me rows of kids, rows of little faces running in face paint and stolen make-up because of the heat, were sitting transfixed by the screen. Rows of hanging little jaws and dull eyes. The air smelt wrong to me: I couldn't concentrate and found after a while that I was gripping the seat arms. On the screen great armies of Fuzzballs of all shapes and sizes were spilling out of the Earth's crust, activated by the unknown emergency. People were welcoming them, saluting them.

I started to estimate how many people the cinema held. About thirty rows maybe and about fifty places in each row. 150? No, idiot. 1500. One thousand, five hundred kids, plus me. I couldn't bring No Machine clearly into my mind any more. *Don't get interested in the sport you bet on*, Dad had written, and look at me: watching the races on TV even when I had no bet down. Losing all my bets. I should have chosen the dogs: *they* weren't on TV.

My eyes itched. I had no idea at all what the story on the screen was doing now. I think that to help us against the threat the Fuzzballs were each finding a human to bond with or something. It didn't make sense. I was so tired, sick. Those witch's words wound through my head:

> *Weary sennights, nine times nine,*
> *Shall he dwindle, peak, and pine*

When I looked along the row the twins were just like the others, mouths hanging open, eyes wide and opaque, not moving at all. All that energy they had, gone. Christ, I felt like I could drink three pints of water. Like when I'd made myself drunk on Dad's rum, just to see. Then my eyes moved nearer, to Hayley . . . and although she was looking at the screen too, she was looking bored.

As I was watching her, watching that thin profile that had been held by the horses on our TV set, she turned her head and glanced at me. And smiled.

'Pretty awful, isn't it?' she whispered. 'Sorry.'

'Pretty awful,' I agreed, smiling back.

'Any chance of some chocolate or a drink or something?'

'OK.'

I found that my legs did still work after all. I fought my way past the knees of the watching kids and went out to the foyer.

The rest of the movie was spent drinking juice and eating popcorn and toffees. Hayley stuffed her toffee wrappers one-by-one in my jacket as she didn't have any pockets.

I couldn't say how the film story ended.

When we'd trick-or-treated backwards down a couple of streets through freezing mist and got back to our doorstep, Hayley said she had to go.

'Isn't your mum coming for you?'

'No, it's only five minutes, silly.'

Beforehand I'd thought that that time after I'd got the twins up to bed might be difficult. Other times when I'd agreed to go out with some girl or other—not often—had made me a pretty good judge of what was expected when. But now Hayley was going and I felt disappointed. Madness.

'Oh . . . Mum said to ask how your dad's job is going.'

'It's going OK. He's still sort-of training. Getting shown the routes and stuff by his boss.'

'Oh. I'll tell her. Well, bye then. Thanks for a lovely afternoon.'

The twins left off counting sweets and bars in their Asda bags and danced round her, crying, 'Hayley, stay, stay, *stay* . . . '

She kissed them and smiled and turned to walk away, but they clung on to her bag and her arm, suddenly desperate, the 'stay's getting longer and more pleading.

I must be a flaming rotten parent, I thought tiredly. I needed to try harder, get it bloody well sorted.

Eventually she got free and said 'bye' again and walked off into the mist.

'Come on then, horrors!' I said, trying to sound like a friend and a dad at once.

As I picked up the abandoned sweet bags and chivvied the girls up to the door, Mr Hermes drove way too fast up the street, banged past a bin someone had left out, mounted the pavement, and went smack into a lamp-post.

5

The car just sat there silently, skewed across the pavement, lights sharply piercing the mist.

The old fool's flaming killed himself, I thought blankly. Or just passed out. He wasn't really an old fool, so I hoped it was that, the passing out.

Nobody else came out onto the street and I envied them. I just wanted to sit in front of the telly or lie in a bath maybe.

'You two, take yourselves up to bed. Hands, faces, and teeth. Get as much of that stuff off you as you can with tissues first. No books. I'll be up when I've helped Mr Hermes, to see you're OK.'

The twins took a last look at the silent car and obediently filed through the door as I held it open, and upstairs. 'Night, Jules. Night, Jules.' Sophie came back down and reached up with her alien cheek to be kissed. 'Night, Jules.'

There was no defence against what I felt for my sisters. It washed through me like pain sometimes.

Our kind neighbour, the old fool Hermes, was in fact OK, already stirring when I got over to the Rover, just a bit shaken up maybe, hopefully.

So Hallowe'en ended—and my fifteenth birthday started—by getting him sorted out with tea and a hot water bottle. And by the end of that week I'd begun to think that maybe I really *was* mad and should dump Liz and get a psy-*chia*-trist instead.

I wasn't going to tell anybody about the birthday, but despite being in shock and not really all there (had he had a stroke or something?—I couldn't smell drink), Mr Hermes knew.

'Tomorrow,' he said vaguely, swaying in the doorway with his key jabbing at the lock. 'The big day, eh, Julian?'

Just then I was breathless and sweating in the cold from pushing his car backwards from the lamp-post and then forward again up onto the flaming drive, while he sat inside and steered.

'Yes,' I panted, 'but it's no big . . . I mean it's not . . . ' *Shit!* I trailed off. As he finally got the door to swing inwards, almost falling inside himself, a great horrible wave of stench poured out and over us.

The *state* of his house!

'Bit of a mess,' he muttered, waving me in. His face under the porch light was a clammy green-white. His thin grey hair hadn't been washed in weeks. Fighting down the wish not to be where that smell was, privately gagging, I took his arm and like a good neighbour helped him inside and up to bed.

When he was settled, I mentioned the police and the doctor, but he said, fiercely, *no* and gripped my arm to look at me and see if I understood. Completely gone, I thought. The kind, neutral hander-out of *kataifi* and a place to get away had fled or gone nuts.

He sank back deeper into greasy yellow pillows and said, 'Right as rain tomorrow. Don't want to trouble people. Just some tea perhaps, lad?'

It was a relief not to be with him for five minutes, but really, that house was like a rubbish tip. Dust and refuse everywhere, old papers, dirty clothes, plastic bags full of crud. Just like one of those old people who never leave their houses and have eighty-seven cats or something, half of them dead, except Hermes had a job and was maybe in his fifties or younger, certainly not older than Dad. And no cats.

The kitchen was worst of all: mouldy tins standing open, rotten milk in cartons, dirty dishes and half-full foil trays from carry-out places standing about everywhere in pools—now solid—of yellow grease.

In June we'd all four come over for a barbecue and the place had been spotless. He'd tried specially to do a Caribbean chicken thing, served on neat paper plates, but too spicy for the twins.

With the cleanest stuff I could find I made tea and took it up.

'You're a good lad,' he said. 'Probably think I've gone potty, eh?' And then, while I made a noise that might have been disagreement, he waved towards a chair in the corner. 'There. Have the little fellow. For your help. A birthday present, if you like.'

On the chair, alone on its broken wicker seat, was a Fuzzball. Unbelieving, I went and picked it up. A purple birdlike thing with one eyebrow raised and crooked orange beak.

'That's Spence, that is,' he said, as if we were still on Planet Earth. 'Not many Spences. Not many made. You're lucky, eh? Very lucky. Had to be Karkos for your sisters, with him—your father—wanting two the same.'

It took a couple of seconds to come up with the right

questions. Maybe old Hermes thought I was just choked up with joy at my Spence.

'Err . . . excuse me . . . are you saying that Dad got those other two Fuzzballs from *you*? . . . And why? . . . I mean, why do *you* have Fuzzballs?'

'Sell the bleeding things, don't I? Whole bleeding region, eh? That's me.'

And that was the last thing Mr Hermes said before slipping into sleep. Holding my birthday present, I stood and watched his face muscles go slack. His mouth hung open and the breath rattled in and out.

Like one of those little glass snowstorm scenes that you can pick up and shake, I still carried images in my head of birthdays with Mum, cake-making and walking and singing and cards that she made herself. And like those scenes I was more than half convinced that my memory was way too sugary, the memory of stuff that never happened quite like that.

Every birthday since Mum had left, Dad had just clapped me on the shoulder at breakfast and said, '(Twelve) are you, boy? Here you are then. Happy Birthday!' and given me a note from his wallet. Only the age ever changed in this ritual.

Dad was a mean bugger and cold and no sort of dad at all, but Mum was driven and had made the deliberately-ugly Self and I probably just invented the sugar because I had to.

I left Mr Hermes to it and went downstairs, taking his cup back to the kitchen, turning off lights as I went.

And then, stepping into one of the downstairs rooms to turn off the light that spilled past its half-closed door, I paused. Alone in the house this one room was immaculate. A big, dark wooden desk, computer left on, stacks of papers, several cork noticeboard things on

35

the walls, loaded with newspaper clippings and photos. Everything dust free and in its place.

I moved closer to the nearest noticeboard.

Every single clipping, picture, and document was about Fuzzballs.

Christ! As well as selling the bloody things, Hermes had gone as nutty about them as the kids themselves.

I killed the lights but left the computer, a 3-D shape rotating slowly on its screen. Closing the door on the stinking house, I crossed back to where the twins were (thankfully) peacefully asleep, each clutching their Karko. They hadn't done too badly with the face paints but we'd need another attack tomorrow.

The Spence I just shoved in the stairs cupboard. Just in case Hermes ever needed proof that I'd kept his gift. I wondered then why he hadn't asked where Dad was, to help with pushing the car and stuff.

All the Fuzzballs had 'special powers'. Did I say that?

The Karkos, it said on their tags, could produce ultra-heat from their eyes, melt you where you stood, and could burrow into solid rock in a blur of teeth and claws.

Other Fuzzballs had shooting sticky tongues, poison-tipped tails, underwater skills or whatever. (One or other of them was bound to be a flaming ninja.)

The card on Spence had said 'clearsight and change'. Obviously Lucky Ferrin's hired hands had run pretty short of ideas by the time they'd come up with powers for the whole range.

All Monday I was on edge.

I was never on edge.

The maths teacher, Shah, said sarcastically, 'Mr Egg,

you appear to have lost us,' in the middle of his lesson. I just looked straight at him for a while without answering and he quickly moved on to talking about something else. *Christ*, wasn't it OK to have an off day for once in his crummy lesson? I wasn't a machine.

At lunchtime I got out the money needed for my next (seventh) bet. £233. I'd already decided that it wouldn't be horses. Dad was right, maybe; I'd got too interested in what I was betting on. It shouldn't have changed anything, of course, because it was all just mathematics, but . . .

I chose a bet of two to one that an in-form David Beckham would score one of the goals for Man. United if they got three or more against Southampton in a cup match that evening. Football bored me to death, so Dad's rules were kept OK.

(The horses were probably getting lined up on Channel 4, snorting white breath and muscle under the pantomime brightness of the jockeys' silks.)

I went back to school and to biology.

Dried beans on the table top.

Miss Pershore, with marking to do, put on a video, a schools programme about the brain and the nervous system. Synapses, miniature gates in our minds, opening and closing to make an infinite number of shapes and patterns. Just like a giant microchip. Except for the little parcels of chemicals streaming through us and carrying what we called emotion and pain and love.

I knew a bit about that already from Liz. It was a con really, having psychiatrists or even psychologists. Depression and madness were just words for when your neuro-chemicals went wrong, out of balance.

Some people believe that life was created on Earth by aliens. I saw it once on TV. Meaning that we're just advanced organic robots or something.

Since the movie, the twins were even more Fuzzball crazy. They didn't play with anything else and screamed and shouted if you took the things away from them. A paper had come back from their school, reminding parents that 'No Fuzzball or Fuzzball-related item whatsoever' was to be brought in.

Deciding I just couldn't be bothered to cook tonight I spent ten minutes making two little signs saying 'CHINESE' and 'OR INDIAN?' with a picture of the flag from each country on the right sign. (Educational too, I thought!) Then I leopard-crawled inch by inch on my belly into the living room, behind the sofa. By stretching hard I was able to get the two signs to appear slowly around the two ends of the sofa, the 'Chinese' one first.

The twins, playing Fuzzballs on the other side, completely ignored my signs.

'HEY!' I called.

Nothing.

It was the kind of stunt the twins would usually have loved. I phoned for a Chinese. Then later, when they were in bed, I watched Scholes and that new Dutch guy score twice each in Manchester's four–nil drubbing of Southampton.

Next morning Hayley was in the car when Mrs Sykes came for the twins. I was an expert by now at getting Sophie and Tanya out at the right time and looking pretty much like human children, although I often had to go up there to their room, these days, to sort them out.

Mrs Sykes said, 'Julian dear, I really need to have a word with your father. Can you ask him to phone me some time this week?'

She knows, I thought. Aunt June filled the horizon.

'My daddy's working. He's away. For a *long* time,' Tanya said seriously.

Sophie nodded. '*Ju*-lian makes spiders and flags with food on an' all that. He's a good daddy too.'

'I'll tell him, Mrs Sykes.' I tried to smile reassuringly over Tanya's head as she clambered in.

From the back seat Sophie, idly playing with Hayley's hair where it spilled over the headrest in front, said loudly, 'Mr Hermes crashed his car! Look!'

Thankfully I talked about the mad neighbour, the old fool, instead of Dad. Told them about his stinking house. Even about the Spence, a mistake which had the twins erupting in the back seat.

'Poor man!' Mrs Sykes said, turning the key. As the car reached the end of our street and turned the corner, Hayley leant out of her window and waved once, watching me.

It came to me that I hadn't seen Hermes since Saturday. The car hadn't moved. What if he'd died in his bed? Probably I should go and see.

I changed into my trainers, got my rucksack, and ran to school, gasping great lungfuls of that traffic-flavoured air. When I came out on to the main road for the last half mile, one of the buses that went that way was just level with me, packed with faces I knew from school, peering out through misty circles. I could imagine the impossible noise and smell in there.

Just leave me alone, I thought, and fought to get well clear of the bus.

'Training for tomorrow? That's right. Good lad.' Hewlett was on gate duty.

Tomorrow, I thought. Wednesday. Oh, Christ . . . Oakwood High. Flaming miles away.

More grief, all day, from Shah and Mrs Lamb and all of them. In the lunch break Curtis had a fight outside the art block, a really vicious one that would have the parents hauled in. (No good . . . it was the two lots of parents that had started fighting first!) I watched the two bodies tearing and kicking and swearing and rolling in the damp leaves

39

on the tarmac and wondered why people gave way to such strong feeling so easily.

You had to cope.

'SPENCE SPENCE SPENCE.' The twins burst out of Mrs Sykes's car and really assaulted me before we'd even got inside.

'WE WANT TO SEE SPENCE!!!'

Did Lucky Ferrin know just what he'd done to our kids?

'Hey, guys . . . how about beeping a little or helping me cook . . . '

But it was no good. I had to show them my Fuzzball while they went pop-eyed and silent with envy and admiration. Then, when I threw it back under the stairs they bustled off to lose themselves in their growing collection of Fuzzball rubbish.

I called after them. 'But this one's mine, OK? No trying to sneak him off to your room.' One Spence without another thing to balance it would cause disaster.

One of them called back, whining. 'That lady done it again like last week. She messed up all our stuff. She been moving our Karkos.'

'Mrs Tanner has just been in to clean like normal, that's all. Come on . . . come down and help me choose a pasta shape.'

When no one came I chose pasta crocodiles. I wondered if Hayley would have known what to say to get them down to help. I wondered if Mrs Tanner could tell from Dad's room that we were a no-parent family now, despite me messing stuff up there on purpose. I wondered if I should forget Dad's system and just try and get a job . . . and when I could find time for that job if I found it.

It took an hour to get to Oakwood, mostly stuck in heavy traffic. I'd forgotten to phone Liz and cancel our session and I had a headache. As the minibus finally bucked over the speedbumps that meant we'd arrived, it started to piss down outside, a steady slanting deluge.

Mr Hewlett said, 'Race starts in twenty minutes. We're a bit later than I thought, I'm afraid.'

Oh, flaming Christ.

At the gun we slithered and slipped off on the slowly rising trail through some thin woods that maybe gave Oakwood its name. As usual I went out well clear. Within two minutes of us starting the freezing rain was plastering my running kit to my skin.

I couldn't make my mind pass into the neutral state that usually took over.

There was no sense of space. I found that I was thinking of my parents. Wondering which one (if either) was sane.

Coming out of the trees and back along the edge of the wood, ready for the second lap, I actually heard breathing at my shoulder and there was an Oakwood kid keeping pace with me. Not allowed. Not to plan. As I glanced back my foot hit a piece of slippery wood hidden under leaves and folded painfully under me, so that I went face first, down into the dirt.

How good just to stay there.

I raised my face to the sky and bellowed like a wild animal into the icy falling drops.

Nothing was the same.

Then I got up and fixed my eyes like a target on the bobbing back of the Oakwood kid and ran like a maniac. A machine. A robot created by flaming aliens.

I ran like Mum sculpted.

When I passed that kid and crossed the line I had tears in my eyes. Hewlett came towards me smiling and I said, 'Go away.' All I wanted was something solid, some peace.

I went straight to the bus and fell asleep, without

41

bothering to change or have team teas. When I woke up we were back at my school, I was shivering, and my ankle was on fire.

I had been too soft with the twins. I wasn't a one-man-show for their oddness and their bloody games.

'Just get out of bed, get dressed, come downstairs, eat breakfast, go to school. That's all you have to do. It's easy. Don't sulk. Don't try to be different. Don't pretend you can't do it.'

I hobbled downstairs and got their bowls of Wheaties. Two bowls the same: the first two out of the cupboard. Being twins didn't mean they were royalty.

Hayley was in the car again and got out this time when the twins got in.

'We hate you, *Ju*-lian,' Sophie said from the back seat. The first thing they'd said this morning, nicely in front of Mrs Sykes.

'What's happening?' I asked when the car drove off and Hayley was still standing next to me.

'Can I walk in with you today?' she asked.

I went back inside, took off my shoe, and sprayed my ankle for about the seventh time with Deep Heat. Hayley followed and watched, looking miserable.

'Can I carry that?' she asked when I got my stuff.

I saw that there was a message on the answerphone in the hall, left while I'd been outside.

'Hello, this is Liz with a message for Julian. You didn't show yesterday . . . just wanted to make sure everything is OK. Give me a call anytime. You've got the number.'

'Who's that?' Hayley asked. I wondered if she was jealous and almost laughed.

'My psy-*cholo*-gist. Which means that I'm not nuts: I just don't cope. In case you wondered.'

I did cope, though. I would tell Liz that I didn't need the sessions any more. I wasn't flaming royalty either, any more than the twins. Time to stop moping and just do the stuff that you needed to do. How hard could it be?

I was angry at how soft I was on myself.

'Come on then,' I said meanly to Hayley, and we walk-hobbled to school in silence, arriving late. But she was just a kid and I was responsible for her—do the stuff that you need to do!—so when I left her to head to physics I said, 'I'm sorry. Come on Saturday again if you want.'

She looked at me hard and again I thought she was going to cry. In the end she muttered, 'Maybe. I don't know if I'm free.'

Physics today was endless experiments with weights and elastic and springs. Everyone knew what would happen. Force, momentum, velocity . . . *gravity* for crying out loud. It was like learning the Latin name for your own toes or something. Did that Man. U Dutch guy know the formulae? Did Beckham study graphs to bend the ball in? Maybe I should offer to teach him? Halfway through I said I needed the toilet and went to phone Liz.

'Can I come this afternoon?'

She said she could cancel somebody else and to come at four.

'Can you tell the school? That I have to leave early?'

She said she would. The school knew about my not coping. They knew I saw Liz. I went home at two and sat at the kitchen table that no longer looked out on to a mess and a silver tree and Self, and drew up a plan for the next week. Shopping needed, when washing had to be done, which bills might need paying. My writing was always very neat, without the letters being joined. I also wrote '£610' on one corner of the paper as that was supposed to be the next bet, if I decided to go on with System 1.

I had ice in my blood. I could see which things mattered.

When I'd made my lists and had the week planned out better than ever Mrs Sykes or someone could do, I lay on the sofa and watched the horses.

Oh flaming Christ.

The tears came again, briefly, and I slept.

When I woke up and had to go to see Liz I couldn't walk at all on my ankle and had to call a minicab. Liz didn't bother with the tea routine. She helped me in and onto the sofa, full of concern.

'Whatever's wrong, Julian?'

'Oh, I just twisted my ankle in the race yesterday. That's why I didn't come by the way . . . sorry. It's nothing, though: it'll go.'

But Liz was shaking her head.

'Not your ankle, silly. I didn't mean that.'

'What then?'

She stared at me and shrugged and went over to the window. Even the psychologist couldn't flaming cope maybe. Maybe I should try to cheer *her* up.

She came back after a moment. 'Listen, Julian, I believe—though perhaps I'm wrong—that you're in trouble of some kind . . . maybe there's a new problem at home, I don't know . . . or you're especially unhappy about something. Of course it's up to you if you don't want to tell me . . .'

I almost laughed.

His bark shall not be lost.

'Can't you do your detective stuff and ask me the right questions to find what you're looking for?'

I didn't mean it to sound so nasty, but Liz was not Hayley and said, with half a smile, 'This isn't psychology. This is an offer of help. Much older than my "detective stuff".'

44

'Help' sounded a pretty nice word, the way she said it. But 'help' would mean Aunt June or social services and all the flaming rest. No way would she put the 'help' above 'professional responsibility' or whatever it was called.

But if I didn't give her something she might try to ring Dad.

I said, 'Can you look after my sisters on Saturday? Dad's away a lot with a new job. I never get time to go out or anything.'

It wasn't something I'd planned, just one of my easy lies, but she bought it and eased off. Perfect. Liz would spend Saturday with the twins in her flat: she'd stop thinking I was some hopeless case now I'd taken her help and given her a reason why I might be up-tight. *And* I could take Hayley somewhere: she and her mum would think it was Dad with the twins so they'd stop hassling too.

Sorted.

Liz still wanted us to have the session.

'What's on your mind this week—apart from not getting enough space?' she asked.

Without thinking much I said, 'Fuzzballs.'

We were back to normal now, she had her bowl of watery tea, I was on the sofa with my ankle propped up.

She laughed. 'Fuzzballs!?'

'Yeah,' I said. 'Ever since the twins got their Fuzzballs they've been useless. They don't play their games any more or help with the cooking or anything.' I'd almost said, 'help *me* with the cooking.'

'Just a craze,' Liz said.

So we talked about that. Crazes. Why those kids had died in Japan. All safe stuff.

In the minicab home I dozed for a minute and when I woke up I knew where I would take Hayley. All that night and the next day I thought about it.

'Well done, Mr Egg. You've come back out of your shell,' Shah said. He could keep his dried beans and his dried jokes and his grey jacket. I was going to see real horses. Racing.

6

'Did you *have* to bring that thing?'

Hayley had her bag open, looking for something, and Spence gazed out at me with his raised eyebrow and his sleek birdlike face. The twins had got him out when she came round in the early morning. She said that he—*Spence*—deserved a trip out too. Was she taking the piss?

'Do you realize, Julian, that the Spences are the most difficult to get? Only a thousand were made. One thousand in the world . . . or was it ten thousand? I can't remember. Anyway, he must be worth loads.'

'Then we'll probably get knifed if we take him.' If he was all that valuable I'd be down the betting shop with him before too long, I thought sourly.

It was the pink Hayley today, though; there was no way she was going to get down now she knew where we were going. And for me too, the steady movement away from home and school and everything made it difficult to let all the heavy stuff hanging over me count for much. Maybe I wouldn't get the train back . . .

I must be crazy.

Apart from the frightening bulge of £610 in my leg pocket, a single betting stake that was more than a quarter of everything we had left, I was also thinking about the For Sale sign that had popped up on Mr Hermes's lawn that morning. The car still dented and unmoving in the drive, everything shut up tight, no sign of the mad old idiot himself, and now that sign. Maybe he *had* died. Maybe it was my fault for not going back to check he was OK.

Too many things to think about. Overload.

Hayley said I was 'daft' when I told her. She said that he'd obviously got better because if he'd died only this week there was no way his house would be so quickly on the market.

Was that logic or just pink reassurance?

'What's Uttoxeter like? Is it a town or what?' she asked for the fourth time. The Sprinter train heaved onwards like a speared bull about to collapse in the ring. Every mile was a relief. I felt like a kid.

'I don't know. I've never been.' I'd never been to any of them, the race-courses, so I chose that place because you could get all the way by train, right up to the course itself. Also, stuck there in the Midlands it might not be too posh and I might not be the only black face. Some of those places on the box . . .

'It's going to be dreamy,' she said happily.

It wasn't dreamy. Not at first sight anyway. After two changes and being squeezed in for the last little train with all the lot I'd hoped wouldn't maybe go to a place like Uttoxeter—suits and those green waxed jackets and everything—we spilled out of the steamy carriage into the same slanting rain that I'd raced in on Wednesday. The countryside, what we could see, was as grey as the sky. Hayley skipped and hopped about and pulled me along to the entrance gates like she was both twins rolled into one. My ankle throbbed and twinged. We bought our tickets and a racing programme—it was only money—and passed through . . . into a different world.

Despite the rain, despite the mud churning up underfoot, the racecourse was humming. A feeling of energy like a million human volts sizzling unseen through the crowds. Glowing eyes, expectation, a special language, something there. *Something*.

We moved slowly forward with the masses, taking it in, and I thought that maybe I wouldn't place a bet today after all. The monkey men at the rails that you see on the box were signing away, waving arms, touching noses, ears, chalking up changing odds on their boards, taking notes from people. But even as we were getting closer to the track, a wave of horses drummed past behind the monkeys, a shining great wave breaking on the finish line and being gently pulled up, calmed down, like dragons or something with their white plumes of breath.

What can I say about that afternoon?

The horses were always there. Totally perfect. Bars and stands and bookmakers were just some sort of ragged fair of hangers-on, side-show nothings . . . with the great beasts moving through it all untainted and untroubled, down to the start, round over the impossible, towering fences in a cascade of heart and muscle and effort, each wave totally blowing away the rest of existence.

Those primeval human volts, a million of them, came from the horses. Any religious cult leader would kill for the buzz and it would still be nothing in his hands.

Had Mum felt something like that, with her stone? Had she tapped into some fizzing electric force she picked up in the air?

Hayley and I stood and watched and wandered and took it all in until I could feel my T-shirt clinging soaking to my skin under the jacket and jersey and Hayley's blue eye make-up was an alien blur over her face. Like drowned rats we found two places to sit up in the stands, warmed our hands on plastic cups of tea, nestled together, a bedraggled Spence wedged between us . . . and finally slipped into muggy half-sleep, washed over and lulled by the ripples of sound as the races went on.

In a half moment of waking, maybe after one of those ripples, I felt Hayley's cheek hot against my face and her small, hard fingers wound into mine. A tiny distant me wondered what I was playing at.

When I woke up, instantly and painfully, that roll of money was burning in my pocket. I knew I had to get a bet down. That's what it was for, for Christ's sake. Where was the problem with that? Just follow the system. The maths couldn't fail.

It was late, though, the cold, drizzly afternoon drawing in. My ankle was worse again and my head throbbed.

'Come on!'

I disentangled myself from Hayley and woke her up. Roughly perhaps, but it was urgent. What if *this* was the race that would get won by the right horse and if I missed it . . .

'Come on! Quick!'

'What . . . ?' she mumbled, squinting. 'What's wrong?'

'I have to see if there's another race.'

And I dragged her down the stands to ground level, while

she sneezed continually and held back and said again, still asleep, uncomprehending, 'What's wrong, Julian?'

There was still a good crowd. There *had* to be another race.

There was.

The first board we came to had eight runners chalked up for a 3.50 race, still twelve minutes away.

Breathing more heavily than the rush down should have caused, I read the list of horses. Great, 2 to 1, something called Tenth Planet. OK, that was the one. I reached for the notes, hot again, my head getting worse.

£610.

Then, also in the list, I saw a horse I knew. Running at 12 to 1 was Slowburn. Slowburn? I tried to call up a picture of him running on TV. A light orangey brown horse, a bay (they called it on the box) with white socks. Yes, I'd definitely seen him win something. Two weeks ago, maybe. I was almost sure I'd liked him. Almost sure that he'd won that race, whatever it was, by bloody miles.

12 to 1! A calmer part of my brain smoothly told me that if he won they'd have to pay me £7320. A single flaming bet that would keep us for half a year, a year . . . ? *Ages*.

Slowburn. I was almost sure he was a fantastic horse. If he was that one I knew, he just couldn't flaming lose.

And so there was my hand in front of me, like something sticking out from one of Mum's statues, alien and misshapen, holding a damp, squashed lump of banknotes.

And my voice, sounding like I was seven, saying: 'All on Slowburn to win, please.'

The man counted the money and gave me a funny look. 'Do you know something I don't then, son?'

Suddenly angry, I said, 'Do you want the bet?'

He narrowed his eyes. 'No. I don't think I do. Not without some ID.'

But further along the rails I found a man who would take the cash and he wrote out a slip. A piece of paper to replace my £610.

In the cold, alone on the kitchen step again, I tried to make sense of the mush.

All I needed to do was separate out the different bits, *strands*, and things would be clear.

I needed to back-pedal a bit, find the clear space again, to get back on top of everything.

I made myself think about the different bits, separately.

First the betting, which had worked for Dad but wasn't yet working for me. And had to soon. Think.

I'd been an idiot today. A mug. Just what Dad had warned about, thinking I knew better than the system. Slowburn had lost—fifth in fact; 'He doesn't much like the softer going, does he?' I heard some poncy, rich idiot say—and even though Tenth Planet had also lost, beaten by a couple of centimetres, I should have chosen him.

And that urgency I'd felt, the desperate need to get the bet down in case this was *the* race where my 2 to 1 shot would make good, that was nuts too. The system didn't work like that. It didn't matter if you waited a whole year for the next bet and all the 2 to 1 horses in that time won. You could pick any race or event, as long as it had the right odds. It was just flaming maths. Dried beans. No urgency.

But the next bet was the last one possible. £1597.

The system, Dad's System Number 1, relied on you having enough money to start, enough capital to cover all losses until you won. The instant you did win you'd always end up with more than you started with, but you never knew how long you'd have to wait for that win.

I'd just have to decide one way or the other. Either to make that last bet, or just write off everything lost and start again, maybe with the same system or maybe with a different one. Not tonight though. Plenty of time to decide tomorrow.

OK, sorted. Think about the twins then.

What about them? Well, it was like the flaming betting. I just had to get on with it. Not get so involved. Of course they missed Dad a bit, but then they didn't know him like I did. And if they knew . . . if they could just *know* what he'd bloody *done*, just pissed off on his own sweet way to the other side of the Atlantic . . . ! But they couldn't know. Not possible. So stop whingeing, Julian, and get on with looking after them. Even if they hate you for it. Don't feel, that's all. Just do the right thing, follow the system. Take charge of the packets of chemicals that we call emotion.

I think they'd been as pleased to see Hayley as to see me, when we went together to Liz's place. Maybe more. And she grinned and tickled and teased and cuddled them while I had to apologize again to Liz for getting back late. I'd already phoned from Uttoxeter, knocked stupid by the loss of that money, trying to make my brain work and produce the right lies about why Dad wasn't back either. Hayley cooed over the kids' drawings while I carefully checked and probed with Liz to make sure no secrets had been given away.

'Remember not to say about Dad being away. In case that lady I told you about has to come and look after us,' I'd reminded them, and they'd looked at me with big, sad eyes and nodded.

Even while she was looking at those drawings, I could sense that Hayley was also half watching me, listening, on to the fact that something was going on, clinging like a pink limpet.

OK. Think about Hayley then. Don't put it off.

My fingertips ran over the rough, cold concrete, brushing tiny chips of gravel. My bum was losing all blood flow.

How had Hayley come into all this?

How had she turned from that young, white-faced kid, into what she was now?

There should be a law against it. There should be government health warnings. Her flaming enthusiasm, her shining eyes, her sleepiness against me on the stands, her anger when I made that bet and she realized how much it was. She came out with words that I hadn't ever heard her use, slapped me hard round the shoulder, asked *why* was I being such an idiot?

And her calm again on the train coming home, prepared not to understand everything about me, gentle once more, pushing in under my arm to rest her head on my chest.

As the clouds gathered and the hassles loomed again, bigger with every stinking mile nearer to home we got, she slept peacefully against me, so close she was just a blur for my senses.

And flaming beautiful.

7

It didn't make sense.

I'd helped sick old Hermes to his bed over a week ago and *nothing* had changed about the outside of that house since then. The smashed car was still there, exactly where I'd sweated to push it. The curtains stayed closed. I was almost sure they were hanging in the same positions—the same exact shapes—from that night. There wasn't the tiniest bit of evidence of anyone living there.

The only thing was that For Sale sign.

I was supposed to be in school in fifteen minutes. The morning was sharp and bright and the one for getting a grip again, taking control like I'd promised myself. No more mistakes racing, or betting, or parenting. And somehow I'd find some way to deal with the Hayley thing.

Anything was possible under that sky.

The twins had been wild again this morning. Wilder than ever. They'd both got their ten metre swimming badges at school last week, and Tanya had been on a 'swimming' thing, breast-stroking and front-crawling her way into the bathroom and downstairs. But Sophie hadn't joined in. She'd got frantic about something, started crying, thrown her bowl of Frosties on the floor, milk and all, uneaten.

Then they'd both flipped, started arguing, going at each other like wildcats, accusing each other of toy-stealing, of messing with each other's Fuzzball stuff.

I'd had to struggle, physically struggle, to give them their kiss goodbye. Mrs Sykes looked fearful as they piled onto the back seat, still quarrelling. She looked as if she wanted to say something to me, but decided not to.

Only eight minutes to go, but it was good standing out here in the winter sun, cold biting through my fleece. Re-taking control didn't mean getting to school on time anyway. Watching out for my neighbours was more important. Just like the betting you had to choose calmly between all the possibles. *Prioritize*, that was the word.

I walked across, leaving our front door still open, and knocked at kind, batty Mr Hermes's door. Then, when nobody answered, I circled the house, going through the side gate to the back and knocking there too, looking up at all the curtained windows and trying to remember which one was the bedroom I'd left the old man in.

Next door to Hermes's I saw someone watching me from her own upstairs window; a woman worriedly pointing at me and then a man next to her, also looking at me.

'Yes?!' I called out to them. Is there a f**king problem? Robert de Niro Egg. I should be able to hold back the flap of my leather coat and show them my piece, so they'd instantly back off.

Why were they pointing like that? They knew who I was, where I lived. Nosy bastards.

'*Yes?*' Christ, they made me angry.

Going back down the side passage, I thought that this must be where the clean room was. That one ordered and carefully arranged and hoovered room in the whole stinking house.

The curtain here was shut too. I tried to remember if it had been shut last week. Probably it had.

'Lucky' Ferrin didn't seem to want to go home. Every news on TV there he was, in the shadows of his car, visiting Stratford, or Madame Tussaud's or some new Nissan plant. Even the races. Like he thought he was a king with his Fuzzball billions.

The huge unsmiling bodyguard said, 'Mr Ferrin has grown to love it here. He feels just like you English are a second *family* to him.' Our family member, Lucky, was apparently to extend his visit until after Christmas; was even considering placing a bid for the Millennium Dome site to make it a permanent theme park for his Fuzzballs and other future creations.

Ponytail said grimly, 'Mr Ferrin would just adore that, to have a base right at the heart of your great country.'

Old obsessed Hermes would be in heaven, I thought. If he wasn't a rotting corpse where I'd left him in his bed.

Maybe some kids had just put that sign in his garden for a joke.

On Wednesday Hewlett took us north and east, almost as far as Lincolnshire. A triangular event: three schools competing together. And good weather for it this time, bright skies and scudding clouds.

Still that weather for taking control.

The other two schools were posh, compared to us anyway. All the kids turned out as if they were going on a school trip, all Mr-flaming-Marvels in their mothers' eyes no doubt. Even when they'd changed they looked different to our lot. Tall, clean-limbed thoroughbreds, niggling at us: our kit, our look, our ratty old bus. They had three or four Nike ticks to every one of ours.

Big deal: ticks didn't make you fast.

I felt just like stretching out on the hillside in the weak sunlight, watching the race instead of running for once. Not a great sign. My mind went like so often now to the horses and I thought of their skittering, pent-up agitation at the start, before they took flight at one million drumming miles per hour. But when the gun went today, nothing in *me* was released.

Basic fitness, hours of circuits, jogging everywhere I went, kept me up with the pack. From there I watched lazily while four or five runners from other schools became strung out in front of us, human stepping stones along the line of flat, pockmarked fields that we were to follow first, before climbing to the low ridge running parallel to our left.

Nothing in me drove me to the front.

Hewlett had gone in his car to the first marking point, a mile and a half down those fields. He was wound up, maybe because I'd skipped extra training yesterday. 'Come on, Egg,' he snapped as I drew level. 'Don't leave it too late, boy. Do what has to be done!' Why did it matter so flaming much to him?

We started on the long elbow-shaped climb to the ridge and with surprise I realized Curtis was right: it hurt.

I think to myself: nothing I have done counts for anything, without this pain. Let me cry for the broken Self. Let me not be the one holding the crowbar. Let me not be spirited away to the land of Aunt June.

A runner from another school, keeping pace at my shoulder, gasps, 'They say you're impossible to bloody beat. Looks like they're wrong.'

F**k you.

And suddenly, in the next moment, he falls away, far below, like I've done a reverse bungee jump high above the earth.

Painfully, gaspingly, knives-in-my-ribs-ingly, ankle-twingeingly, I up the rate of my footfall, pick my knees up a little higher, make the balls of my feet springy and relaxed. Grindingly, I enter a no-man's land between the labouring pack and the ones strung out ahead.

Yes, I was right; the chemical packets—the streams inside—CAN be diverted, with sweat, with huge effort. Not total control, not the clean, dry decisions of my father: but a blundering, hopeful, painful half-control.

I fight for the ridge summit, locking each knee open at 180 degrees before it's allowed to bend again, pushing hard off the earth. At the top the breeze carrying those clouds is cold in my face and on my imploding chest, but I fix the kid in front, forty metres off, and make sure that my feet hit the ground more often than his. I am at his shoulder when we come off the ridge for a plunge back down to the valley floor and then go slithering, sliding, leaping well ahead, not thinking or caring about the risk of turning that weakened ankle once more.

Hewlett has driven on again and is at the third marking point, at the base of this descent.

Lighting a pipe he says, sarcastically, 'What's this then? Julian Egg and his impossible comeback?' He doesn't want effort, just a result. F**k him, too.

Another flat section, this time through a thin wood, trainers exploding among the dry leaves. I cannot see the next target, two runners together, because of the trees and the bending path. I set a fast rhythm in my head and make the leaf explosions *match it, so that on leaving the trees I am almost up with that pair.*

My heart will explode.

More markers, then another climb, much steeper than before with parts of the route giving way to bare stone and gravel, back to the ridge summit where we are to go across and immediately over, dipping back down to the start/finish in one long stretch.

For the second climb I bug the hell out of the pair in front by staying only a pace at their backs. They respond with gasped, spat-out abuse over their shoulders; racist and very very dull: I've heard it before. This run is a shape waiting for me to find and unlock by my effort, desire, need: even if the shape turns out not to be perfection.

At the summit I leave the pair cleanly, making sure that an immediate twenty-metre gap squashes ideas of using me as pace-maker to the finish. For a few strides I look down across a glittering sweep of fields, then the acceleration to terminal velocity slip-sliding diagonally down the hill, entering the last field at the back of one of the two guys still ahead: crossing the line a hair's breadth in front of him.

Hewlett has again arrived first. He makes the best of it with bad grace. 'Well . . . second isn't bad. Better than it might have been. Just don't understand why you couldn't do that from the start.'

I am on my hands and knees, almost seeing white with the recent effort, trying to breathe in half the air in the world.

Nothing was quite the same now.

I went to bed at nine or ten in the evening and slept heavy ten-hour sleeps, hardly able to talk in the mornings as I poured Frosties for my sisters.

I was more like a child, a new baby, than the person who would feed and provide for two whirlwinds of innocent unpredictable life. Otherwise I would become pinched, wasted, a skeleton, eventually only a single pellet of steel. Like Schwarzenegger in that movie, losing all the bits that make him seem human.

I wandered around in my socks, eating cereal bars, going over and over what was important in my mind, to stay focused. The garden, when I looked out, was a perfect white, frosted square.

At school I started doing worse in Maths, but better in English. Madness. Probably my blitzed childlike self was just what Mrs Lamb wanted. Feeling my way through the words.

Though his bark cannot be lost . . .

A million things were easier, though they had seemed simple before. Other things became mountains, new to me.

'What *is* it, Egg?' Hewlett asked irritably after I'd struggled round the training circuit the required ten times.

'I don't know. Maybe still the ankle. It'll pass,' I told him. Just get off my case, Hewlett.

It seemed now that I'd been wound tight as a guitar string *before* and that the string had snapped. The slackness in me prevented worry, prevented achievement, even prevented anger.

For two weeks following Uttoxeter, Hayley was not allowed to see me outside school hours, punishment for coming back late. At school she seemed changed too— though how could I be sure of anything?!—the chalk-white version of her no longer making any appearance. It was good we couldn't meet outside school. I was working out my own new system for the betting. Putting several bets on each day, but small ones. Usually accumulators, where each time you won your money went into another bet (so that £1 could win you thousands if you got it right), or bets that horses would just get a top-three-or-four placing. It all worked on percentages, like everything. If I could get a job (when?!) or make some money I'd go back to the first system maybe, but for now I still got the same buzz, almost the same, without the guilt and the heart failure.

I was learning more, too, about 'form' and what that idiot had meant about 'soft going' and everything. Taking control. Before the money went I'd know enough to keep the three of us. I wrote down all the bets and the results systematically to study the patterns. Use the dried beans for something worthwhile for a change, I thought.

In the shops the Fuzzball displays were tinsel-covered monoliths, dwindling to nothing and being re-built daily. It was as if nobody wanted to give or receive anything for Christmas *except* Fuzzball products. Father Christmas must be tearing his flaming beard. Records were set by various kids on the news for the size or scope of their Fuzzball collections. Daily TV cartoons, animated badly by computer in Japan, dubbed over with American voices, kept the child population of Britain addicted.

It was good being able to park the twins in front of that crap while I worked on my bets.

Sometimes I ended up telling Liz things just to stop her asking about other things. This was one of the parts that wasn't as easy as it used to be. Most of all I had to keep her away from stuff to do with home and Dad.

'Julian,' she said, 'I haven't been paid in quite a while. It's not a problem, if your father's finding it hard at the moment or just forgotten maybe, but get him to give me a call sometime, will you?'

How long until Mrs Sykes asked again—insisted probably with the way the twins were now—to speak to Dad? I could imagine her just marching straight in, brushing me out of the way: 'Mr Egg? Donald? It's Cynthia

Sykes here. *So* sorry to disturb you, but we really *must* talk about your daughters. I'm so *worried*, really I am, Mr Egg . . . . Hello? Mr Egg? . . . Coooey?'

I'd have to work something out.

Liz waited for my reply, so I said, 'Sure,' and then, quickly . . . anything: 'Did you like Hayley . . . that girl I was with the other day?'

Christ.

'Oh. Yes. She seemed very nice. Very good with your sisters, isn't she? Is she your girlfriend?'

Pause. Sinking.

'Sort of, yeah.'

Liz smiled. 'You're lucky then!'

I thought about that with surprise. Yes, I guessed from Liz's or someone outside's point of view I probably was lucky. They probably didn't realize how it messed things up. Complicated them. But it was true: Hayley was pretty in her way and loyal and good with my sisters; and liked me for some reason.

Liz said, wryly, 'You don't *look* very happy about it. Don't you like her?'

I thought of Hayley's smell. Of her eyes flashing when she cuffed my shoulder about that bet. It frightened me.

'I don't know why she likes me. It doesn't make any sense.'

'Oh yes? And why's that, exactly? You're a good-looking young man. Intelligent. I'm sure lots of girls like you. Fifteen years ago I'd have fancied you myself, I expect. What is there not to like?'

She sounded off-hand, but I knew her and knew when she asked questions she thought were important.

'Well, I'm *here* for a start, aren't I?' It came out angry and childish, like I was sorry for myself, which I wasn't.

Liz let me hear myself and then said, quietly, 'Hayley—if that's her name—didn't seem daft to me. She seems like a girl who knows her own mind. If she likes you there must be a reason. So . . . hmmm . . . you *could* just trust her instincts . . . or, alternatively, you could ask her what it is that she likes about you.'

It seemed so easy, so simple. Was it really that easy?

We talked some more. The nothingness to pad out what had gone before. Wrapping the wound in cotton wool. I mentioned the Fuzzballs craze again: the fact that I was worried how hooked Sophie and Tanya were.

I asked, 'If our emotions and feelings and everything are just groups of chemicals, why do people suddenly behave differently? And why do lots of people sometimes go mad at once, all spending their money on junk like that?'

Liz said, 'I'm not sure that our emotions and feelings *are* just groups of chemicals. That's like saying music is just vibration of the air, or your favourite book is just black marks on white paper. The chemicals are just the nuts and bolts that express and respond to a huge range of stimuli.'

Her and her fancy language. 'So we *can* control them then?'

She looked at me strangely. 'We can . . . encourage them, perhaps, in one direction or another. Is that what you think these sessions are for with me? To get more control?'

I didn't answer.

'Maybe . . . ' she said, 'maybe these sessions are to learn to control *less*, Mr Julian Egg. What do you think of that?'

I didn't see that. It was barking mad. People who didn't cope—not that that meant me, anyway—needed to get more of a grip, not less.

I went back to the last subject. 'So what would you do about Hayley, if you were me? Ask her?'

64

'No,' my psychologist said; 'I'd trust her instincts. And yours.'

As usual we just went in flaming circles. Waste of time.

It just made me tired, really drained.

Every day I knocked at Hermes's front and back doors. I phoned the estate agents, Davies and Crisp, and asked what they could tell me.

'And your name is?'

'I'm just someone who knows him. I was worried, that's all, seeing that sign. Is he OK?'

'I'm sorry. I really can't discuss the private affairs of a client. I'm sure there's no need for you to worry.'

One night, as I watched the house, sitting near my window upstairs, I saw a light. I thought I saw a light. Just briefly, playing over the side fence, down where the 'clean' room was.

When I went across, in trainers and dressing gown, there was nothing.

I knocked and called.

I wasn't even sure if the curtains had changed a little, in that room. Not even when I looked in daylight the next morning.

8

Liz reminded me of Mum, thinking like she did, trying to see the good in everything. Or was that just the chemical streams and little packets of memory getting confused? Like déjà vu or something.

Like the twins' mum later, Mum had been a student at Dad's college when they met. She rode a wartime wreck of a bicycle to lectures, with long striped scarves to keep her warm. For her first year she was right in with the arty student lot, drinking lapsang souchong and tearfully arguing politics and social issues. Against all mathematical probability Dad magnetized her out of there, after she had entered his classroom by mistake one day, and soon set her up in his home . . . where his bald, dry, logical certainty, which had seemed so thrilling and different and exciting when they met, started to starve the life out of her.

Even though she packed college in, she carried on with her sculpting; and each creamy, grainy cube of oolite that arrived became a new tank of oxygen. A new life-shape waiting to be discovered, imprisoned in the stone till she set it free. Her words. She told me that she never really chose what it would be: it was more like join-the-dots or magic painting. As Dad gradually put off each of Mum's friends from ever visiting, she became a single figure in her white snowstorm scene.

Almost a single figure anyway. The new baby—me—lay next to her in its limestone-dusted pram and was soothed by the tapping chisel, freeing the inevitable form of the stone.

If my feelings were tiny packets of chemicals in the brain, could I decide to change the contents of those packets? Without some psychiatric drug like Prozac, that is. Or was I helpless to the chemical streams within?

'A spokesman for the Treasury,' the TV said, *'today confirmed that the consortium headed by Fuzzball billionaire Lucky Ferrin has been given the status of "preferred bidder" for the Millennium Dome site. Mr Ferrin issued a statement expressing his delight and denying that the gift of Fuzzball products for Cabinet members had anything to do with this decision.'*

The newsreader raised an eyebrow like Spence so you knew this part was a joke in his script.

I was an oolite cube myself.

Was the shape inside already clear and formed or could I take control?

The neat patterns that had run through my life no longer existed. In circuit training my lap times were hopelessly erratic, so that Hewlett rolled his eyes and talked about me being 'preoccupied' or 'disturbed'.

By what, though?

He said, heavily, 'I've put your name in for the area junior cross-country trials on Friday 11th December, by the way. That's the second Friday in December: make sure you write it down somewhere. If transport's a problem I can run you down there myself.'

At home there were days when I was empty of ideas for the twins and empty of patience or desire to care for them. But when we'd finished doing their reading homework together—one on each side of me on the sofa—I'd find myself saying, 'What shall we read now?' or 'OK, folks . . . it's *bath time*!' Bath time meant half an hour getting clean and forty minutes cleaning up afterwards.

One morning a letter came for Dad from their school. Would he go in some time soon to talk about their behaviour at the moment? Would he phone to make an appointment? The same morning—what was the mathematical probability?—there was also a letter from *my* school. '*A worrying percentage of lessons missed* (it said) . . . *aware of a difficult background . . . an appointment for an informal talk about his future.*'

Cold with anger at the nosy, interfering bastards, and anger at myself for letting this happen, for not playing the game better, I missed more lessons and messed around with a cassette player, practising phone call voices and what kind of stuff to say, half watching the horses skidding about through thick mud at Towcester races. Then when I was ready I made the calls.

A piece of piss. Speaking as Dad, I got appointments to talk about my children three whole weeks from now; plenty of time to let the hassles die down and think of something else.

When the twins were home, I asked them about school.

'What's going on? Why do they want to see Dad? What have you been doing there?'

They pulled away.

'Nothin'. We haven't done nothin'.'

'I'm tired!'

'Can I have some Coke?'

'Get *off*, *Ju*-lian.'

They wouldn't meet my eye these days. They seemed suddenly old and cynical and impossible to pin down. They lied as easily as me. I hardly knew them. They seemed deflated and desperate, like all the magic had gone out of their lives.

Too early, I thought, *please let them keep their magic a while longer*.

I stood at the bottom of the stairs and shouted, 'We've got to sort this out!'

Saturday was two weeks since the races (two weeks since freedom!) and so Hayley's ban was over.

I was going to play it cool.

The house was tidied that morning and the twins were forced into a bath full of bubbles and there was food to offer her. I was going to be the same Julian Egg that had made her blush for the last year or more. The one that coped and won his races. The real Julian Egg. If we were going to end up doing the boyfriend/girlfriend thing it would be on my terms.

'Hi,' she said, uncertainly, standing on the step.

'Hello, Hayley. Come in. How's it going?'

She was all in black, which was something new to me. Except she had silver trainers and when she took off her coat there was writing on her black top, also in silver. It said *Extreme Babe*. I thought maybe there was something different about her hair too.

For the first time in days the twins had one of their things, crazes, themes . . . whatever. Princesses. Not

Fuzzballs. They swept down the stairs with feathers and plastic jewels in their hair, wrapped in net curtains over pink leotards.

Hayley caught on at once, of course.

'Oh, your royal highnesses! Your majesties! How beautiful you are!'

'Yes!' they agreed. 'We *are* very very beautiful. Kiss our hands, if you want.'

Hayley curtsied and kissed their hands and suggested that in the afternoon if they had glue and all that, she could help make them some rings and necklaces, beautiful enough for such lovely princesses. They giggled and batted their eyelashes and I thought it was just flaming typical that today of all days they'd decide to act all wonderful and little-girly instead of what they were like the rest of the time.

'Lunch first,' I said.

'Rings first!' they shouted.

'No. I said lunch. We'll have lunch first.'

They were going to be shitty after all.

'Come on,' Hayley said, taking a princess on each side. 'Why don't we decide what sort of rings and things you want while we sit and eat?'

And somehow the day was lost before it had started. Whatever I did, I ended up looking as if I didn't know how to deal with my own sisters and flaming Hayley charming them and giggling away with them as if she was six too. She didn't have a bloody clue about all the cooking and shopping and washing and cleaning up. She was still in a kid's world. It was easy for her.

I was right to make more space between her and me, I thought. I didn't want to go out with some kid.

While they played together upstairs I sat and watched the horses. I had eleven small bets on this afternoon, placed quickly first thing, while the twins were glued to the box after breakfast. Horse after horse running for me, trying its best, snorting and sweating and straining towards the finish. *They* were worth loving. If they let you down it was just because you didn't give them the right food or training, or because they were ill, I thought. They were a better bet than people. Through spreading the money round and never betting more than a fiver at a time on one horse, I was only losing at a rate of 25 per cent overall now.

Occasionally, I panicked at the sinking money level on the cash machine display. A great black hand on my throat was what it was like. But the moments passed: I was getting there. Down to just 25 per cent loss.

'Princess Sophie and Princess Tanya would like to go to ye royal park,' Hayley said from the doorway, the girls chattering and singing away behind her.

'So go,' I said. Perhaps it came out hard-sounding, but she hardly needed me, did she?

She came over and stood behind where I was sitting on the sofa. She rested her small hand on my shoulder. 'Don't you think that as Lord Chancellor, you should go with their royal highnesses?'

I turned off the box and got my coat.

Despite myself, it was good watching the twins bombing down the slide and shrieking with fear as I hauled the roundabout harder and harder. At the end I agreed to be a dragon, ravening after the princesses with my great plumes of frozen breath-smoke and chased them home.

At five, when the twins were exhausted in front of the TV, Hayley said abruptly that she had to go. She said that and immediately opened the door, let herself out into the dark, and started walking away down the street.

I went on the step and called, uncertainly, 'Did you have a good day?'

'No.' She stopped and turned, standing under the streetlight. Were there tears on her face? 'No. It was rotten. Just like you wanted.'

So even after she'd left she found a way to tie me in bloody knots. Controlling every situation. Always keeping me off balance. Why do girls do that?

I guess Dad didn't stand a chance against Mum. No wonder he had to smash that statue.

Sleep didn't really come at all that night. Funny after the ten-hour total zonk-outs I was usually having now. There were so many things I wanted to just let go of and none of them would let me. Liz, school, the twins, Hewlett with his area trials, and Hayley—who *pretended* not to make any demands!—worst of all. Of course I didn't really want to let go of the twins, though. Out of the whole clinging, leeching bunch *they* were the only ones not to blame. And somehow they were the ones I was failing the worst. Seeing them with Hayley . . . well, I'd kind of thought that maybe the Fuzzball craze or something was making them mental, but they'd been OK today. So it was me. Or missing Dad.

Me.

I needed to re-focus just on the important stuff. I was still trying to deal with too much, getting distracted by things, even if it wasn't my fault. Sometimes I thought it would be a relief if I could just tell someone how hard it was, being a parent and everything. But then I knew from Liz that talking never sorted anything out, not really. You just had to work it out yourself and be strong.

I *was* strong.

As the night went on I dozed a little, flipping between consciousness and unconsciousness every few minutes.

She'd pinned her hair back a bit, in sort-of half moons, away from her cheeks. I loved her movement: it was simple and effortless, sure and beautiful. She seemed so strong, although her bare arms were so thin and her shoulders so narrow.

I surfaced heavily, sweating, aching. It was my heart aching. I didn't want to be awake: I wanted to dive down again, to where I could be with her safely. But something had woken me. Something, at the edge of my awareness. Something . . .

Oh God. Let me just dive down again and forget . . .

Then . . . . *then* I was coldly and completely awake. It was something to do with Mr Hermes, something to do with the house opposite that had woken me. Something that had reached me in the aching, painful green depths. I swung out of bed and felt in the darkness for some jeans, then went to stand at the window, pulling the curtain back a couple of millimetres to look. I realized that my heart was beating fast, like on the starting line.

Nothing was moving under the orange pools of light. Just white frost-gripped cars, sitting in cold silence. Nothing was moving opposite either. An ugly, square, brick house with darkened windows and a dented car in the drive. And then my senses screamed, tracking in on what was different. No mistake this time. There was the tiniest line of illumination along one edge of Hermes's front door. Not a reflection—nothing there to reflect, just stained wood—and nothing that I had seen before, the times that I'd watched.

I felt a sudden savage joy. OK, you bastards, *this* I could handle. My three possible choices were spread out for me, untangled and perfect. I could call the police, anonymously, which meant a call box several streets away; I could go back to bed and sink again into sleep, where anything might happen; or I could go and see what was going down opposite.

The twins were safe and asleep, unmoving as light from the landing fell on their faces. I carried my trainers downstairs to put them on, then found the handle to Dad's snooker cue: a present from the twins' mum, made of Nigerian hardwood, black and dense and glinting with mother-of-pearl.

Then I went across the street.

It was freezing and clear, and my body moved easily. I hadn't bothered with a shirt. I felt like I did in my races. I could run one now and nobody would be able to touch me.

Again at the front door the choices came clearly to me. Either to carry on quietly, to move through the house room by room until I made sure there was no threat, nobody attacking old Hermes or robbing him, or to charge in and make sure that any surprise was on my side. I shivered and tensed up to go for it, gripping the half-cue more firmly where it was already sticky with sweat from my hands.

Then I re-thought the probabilities, counted in my head how many rooms I'd have to get through in one charge and how long that would give any intruder. And also, if it was just Mr Hermes in there, if there was no problem and he'd just forgotten to close his door properly . . . well, I could give him a heart attack, charging in there with my weapon. It almost made me laugh, imagining it.

The door was a fraction open, as I'd seen from my room, and a light was on in the hall. I reached out until my finger tips rested gently on the cold wood. I tried to remember if this door creaked at all, when you opened it. No, it swung easily inwards: slowly, though, not losing contact with my fingers.

The hall was bright under an unshaded bulb, glaring down on the filthy carpet. The stench from before was still there, worse than ever. I decided to move right to the top first, to check on old Hermes's bedroom. Helping him was the first thing, if he was here and hurt in any way.

He wasn't.

Nobody was here. Not now. But they had been. *Somebody* had been in this house.

Like I said, the whole place was still the same tip, only worse. The kitchen and toilet ten times worse, making me gag again.

The important change was in the 'clean room', the last I looked in as I worked my way back towards the front door.

That, too, had become a tip. A real chaotic mess, all the papers and diskettes and folders thrown in heaps on the floor, the noticeboards also torn down, and the computer gone. The wires still trailed over the desk where they'd just been ripped free. And over the top of everything, a smell that was new in this house: cigarette smoke.

I went and shut the front door again. It was just a Yale lock, but I should get some warning if *they* came back. Then I went back into the 'clean' room and sank down onto the floor, next to the mess of papers. Without knowing what I was looking for, I started to sort through them.

I don't remember it happening, but at some point in that room I must have dozed off again, because I was suddenly aware of morning light starting to show through the curtains . . . and that I was colder than I'd ever been. My teeth were chattering, my head splitting, my muscles locked stiff.

I looked at the sea of stuff over the floor. I'd hardly touched a third of it and I needed heat right now, so I just took one thing that seemed worth some thought and decided to come back later, maybe tonight, for a better search and to bring anything else home.

It was more difficult now, with the cold gripping every part of me, to see the choices clearly. Not like during the night. Vaguely I was aware that the police would have to be called at some stage. Somehow that would have to be done without saying who I was and where I lived. The lies needed would take some time to construct, but if I got them wrong then social services would be next. But also, I was excited, deep down. Really excited. There was something here to discover, something flaming *massive*, to do with the Fuzzballs. I wasn't clear exactly what yet but whatever it was, old decrepit Hermes with his sugary pastries had known about it and was now missing.

Taking my one item, I killed the lights in Hermes's house and fixed the front door so it looked closed but could be opened again later with a push, by leaning a chair against the inside. Then I headed back across to my house. A car started along the street—someone taking their dog for an early trip to the urban park or going for their papers perhaps—and I thought what a strange sight I must be; naked to the waist in a freezing dawn.

Believe me: it was a moment of pure sodding ecstasy when I sank into a deep, hot bath. Again, my senses went out of focus and sleep took me.

After their 'good' day yesterday, the princesses were really hyped up and wanted more of the same. Making things, cutting out and gluing, dressing up, all that stuff. I wasn't good at art and making my hands do careful things, but started off OK with them and for a while we all sat peacefully at the kitchen table with our mess of glitter and glue and shiny paper and dried rice.

I was good at caring for them. It felt good, too. I'd

just been too tough on myself, too much like the Schwarzenegger metal skeleton. I was easily as good as Hayley: and *I* did all the difficult parts of looking after two children, too. For the first time in what felt like months Sophie, Tanya, and I were comfortable with each other, and I was hopeful that we could last out. Another year, maybe, and then I'd be sixteen, out of school if I wanted, and the social people might let me take care of my sisters officially. Or would I have to be eighteen for that?

I was proud that in the night I'd known what to do. It made me think again that there was nothing I couldn't cope with. When the pressure was really on, I came up with the goods. All the rest, all the phantoms and imaginings about stuff that could go wrong, that was all shit. That was the world where Liz lived, full of cobwebs and fantasies, trying to sound like science.

To celebrate properly knowing this again, after forgetting it for so long, I decided to make pancakes for lunch. Banana and honey maybe, with some nuts or something on top. I was humming to myself, that tune from the Ford ads, and when the mix was ready I decided to call Hayley and invite her too. She could see us on a good day, for a change. Also, I wanted to tell her about my night; see what she thought.

'Hi,' I said. 'Hi, Hayley? It's Julian.'

'Oh . . . hello, Jules.'

She sounded miserable. Poor girl: it would be enough to make anybody flaming miserable living with that bossy, nosy mother, I thought.

'Um, I'm just going to cook lunch. It'll be done in twenty minutes. D'you want to come and eat with us?'

'I don't think so.'

'OK. Well, afterwards, then, if you want? Come this afternoon.'

She said, 'Why, is your usual babysitter on holiday?' It almost sounded angry.

I said, 'What's up? Is there anything wrong?'

'No,' she said. 'Everything's just fine. I expect we'll see each other at school. Bye.'

She didn't stay on the line long enough for me to say anything else.

Well, fine to you too then, I thought. We'll have our flaming pancakes without you and you can just sulk your day away about whatever it is eating you. You're not going to spoil another of *our* days.

As I went to put the phone back on its charging thing, I caught the bowl of pancake mix with my elbow so that it went crashing to the floor. Broken earthenware and thick yellow mix.

'Shit,' I said and threw the phone against the wall, as hard as I could. Behind me, unseen, Sophie had come into the room. When I turned and saw her she just stood looking with those big, frightened, round eyes.

'What?' I said. *'What?'* and she ran off down the hall.

9

Something crazy was going on. If Sunday hadn't turned into such a stinking day (if Hayley hadn't reached into our house and somehow managed to turn a good day on its head) I would have stayed switched on and maybe got to the craziness.

Sunday night, though, I just crashed out on the sofa as soon as the girls were in bed, and then the next thing was that it was Monday morning and we were right back into the week's routine, charging about the house trying to beat Mrs Sykes's horn and my own class register. Whatever happened, we had to be in at school at the right times and not in any trouble for the next three weeks. I'd told the twins: threatened them again with the Aunt June they'd never met, and hoped it was enough to keep their wildness limited to when they were at home.

And so I missed my chance.

Hayley must have been avoiding me at school: I hardly saw her, and never got close enough to talk. She was making sure that groups of friends were around to insulate her. Fine, I thought: I had things to do anyway. When the last lesson ended I was first out of the gates and running along to Boots to get a new phone. Then on to the gnome in the betting shop to check the rest of my Saturday bets. That was a mistake: they were a total wipe-out. I'd lost more-or-less all of them this time. ('Had enough yet, Sonny Jim?' the old fart wheezed happily. 'Wish we had more like you! Nineteen, eh?' . . . 'No, twenty now. You asked my birthday, remember?' Mean old bastard. Trying to trip me up: he'd have to do better than that.) By four twenty—well ahead of Mrs Sykes—I was home, ready to get some bin bags and bring all Hermes's papers and stuff over the road where I could take more time sorting them out.

I was pretty sure that the nosy pointing couple next to that house were both at work in the afternoons.

They could've been out on the lawn with telephoto lenses, though, and a marching band. Because at last, today of all days, there was a change in that house. The car had gone. And the sign . . . the sign said *SOLD*.

All the curtains were back. No, not back, just missing.

In a dream, I walked across. The door was open. I pushed it and went in, and saw . . . nothing. Really nothing. No curtains, no light fittings, no carpet, no possessions of any kind. Only the very faintest trace of that smell from before, still lying under a new mixture of fake, chemically pine, and flowers, and lemon.

Everything was spotless, totally clean and empty. Including the 'clean' room.

I wandered out into the hall and then along to the kitchen—same story there: the whole place must have been bleached to get it so clean—and a voice said, 'Yes? Can I help you?'

Behind me was a man in a black or very dark suit. He

was maybe thirty, compact-looking, and his eyes were as dark as his suit. Everything about him looked expensive and smooth and made my stomach churn.

I asked, 'Who are you? Where's Mr Hermes? What's happened here?'

He looked at me coldly and said, 'I am Mr Crisp. I am an estate agent. Do you know what that is, young man? It means that I sell houses. It does not mean that I am an information service. Today, I have sold *this* house. And that means that it belongs to somebody, and that *you* are trespassing.'

What a wanker! What a way to talk! I could quite happily have smashed his sneering, so-superior face in. But I took a breath or two . . . and just left as he wanted.

Then, being extra smart or perhaps plain stupid, I went along the street instead of just over, and came back from the other way, having jogged round the block.

Mrs Sykes's car was already there, of course, when I got back. I wondered, seeing her standing outside our door, why every last piece of luck seemed to have deserted me so totally. Like some god was toying with me, seeing how much I could take.

'Ah, Julian,' she said icily. 'I was starting to think that nobody lived here any more.'

'No. That's OK. I was just doing some extra training. Sorry, Mrs S.'

She wouldn't leave. 'No, it is *not* OK, Julian. At first I welcomed the fact that your father had work at last. I was determined to help out, if I could. But I don't believe I've set eyes on the man for . . . well, God *knows* how long: it *feels* like weeks or even months, though I dare say it can't be as long as that.'

Yes, I thought. It can.

'I have also *phoned*,' she went on, '*several* times. [True,

81

six times to be exact, but what was I supposed to do about those messages? I could hardly pretend to be my dad on the phone to Mrs Sykes, who knew him so much better than the school secretary.] I would like you, assuming that the man is *not* here at this moment . . . ? [I shook my head] I would like *you* to convey my worry at how little time he seems able to spend with his family. Maybe he would call in to discuss this with me? This is something more than just a polite invitation, as I'm sure he'll realize. Heavens, if it weren't for Hayley having seen him herself, I could easily believe that he's just disappeared off the face of the earth.'

Mrs Sykes got in the car and drove off.

'We did good?' Sophie whispered to me, questioningly, sadly.

'Yes,' I said. 'You've been very good. Perfect.'

I gathered them to me in a hug. Tanya started to cry, softly. I held them close, my wonderful sisters. It was difficult to fight back the tears myself. I was being squeezed, flattened against the earth by unseen weights.

Somehow I'd find a way.

None of those bastards out there would get to us. Nobody would mess with my family.

In my mind I almost thought of Hayley as one of them, one of the bastards, interfering and squeezing the life out of us. But then I remembered what Mrs Sykes had said—*if it wasn't for Hayley having seen him herself*—and I had to re-think. Maybe she was one of *us*, after all. It was difficult, though, to feel grateful. If she *knew*, for Christ's sake, then why . . . ?

But I wasn't sure really what the question was.

The three of us went in the house and I got the twins juice to drink in front of the box, one in a pint mug, one in a wine glass. They sat holding hands, sipping their drinks, and I went to get the thing I had taken from Mr Hermes's house on Saturday night.

But I couldn't even find that.

Needing some release, whatever got done to us, I cut out of school at lunch the next day and put fifty quid on something called Dab Hand to win in the 3.30 at Doncaster, breaking my new set of self-imposed betting rules. Dab Hand was a real character, sometimes bursting his heart to win and sometimes deciding just to do his own thing. When he motored, he had what they call a long, grass-cutting action. Awesome. Today he was only at odds of 7 to 2, as last time out with this jockey, he'd dumped the guy on one of the fences.

The rest of the day I sat in my place in the different lessons and racked my brains about the item—a sheet of paper—that I'd lost. First trying to think of places I hadn't looked—I'd been knackered and freezing when I'd got in after all, so I could have thrown it anywhere—and then trying to re-create the information on a new piece of paper.

The implications, if I hadn't really 'lost' that paper, were so large that I couldn't think of them yet. So I concentrated on what had been on it. Which was basically a picture, or diagram, of a molecule.

A molecule is a group of chemicals bonded together to make a larger chemical building block. For example, you could have a molecule of water, which is H_2O: that's two hydrogen (H) atoms joined together with one oxygen (O) atom. Whether atoms will join with each other to make molecules depends on the 'shape' of the atoms—like how many electrons they have. And when you make a diagram of a molecule, you can see how each atom joins with the rest, using little bridges. Water, which is a really simple one, would look like this:

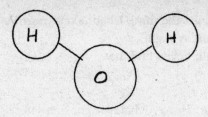

H_2O. That's two hydrogen atoms joined to one oxygen atom.

The paper I'd got from Hermes's stinking, burgled house had a diagram of a molecule, but a really complex one: not at all like water. Mostly to show complex molecules properly you need a 3-D model, which you make from lots of coloured spheres (the atoms) kind-of plugged together like a puzzle; and I had the feeling that this particular diagram was a 2-D print-out of a 3-D computer picture. Rows and rows of atom-spheres and bridges to connect them. Hundreds of the things maybe.

Whatever, it was definitely a print-out. It had said at the top that it was an e-mail: sent to hermesk@aol.com by somebody called Dougie, with a date about three weeks ago. For some reason it didn't give Dougie's e-mail address.

Finally, across the bottom of the paper, somebody had written clumsily in pencil, something like: *'Is this it? The tiny thing that keeps them hooked?'* I wasn't sure of the exact words, but that part wasn't part of the print-out so the person who'd written it must have been Hermes himself.

And now I didn't have that paper any more. Which left me getting more and more wound up as I tried to repeat the complicated diagram from memory.

'Thank you . . . *I'll* have that, I think!' Shah said as he materialized next to my table and whipped the latest effort out of my fingers. 'Chemistry, is it? Well, boy, this is *maths* you're in now. From what I hear, you need to keep your wits about you at the moment! Eh?'

He screwed up the paper, my best try yet, and threw it away. *Keep my wits about me!* That was a good one. A good flaming joke. The amount of stuff I had to balance and deal with every day, while he just chundered on with his stinking quadratic equations . . .

Remembering the appointment Dad had to see the Head, I made my brain pass into the grey soup needed for Shah's little world.

One thing couldn't really be escaped from, even if I didn't choose to think about it now. Which is that however done in and freezing I'd been coming back home on Sunday morning, I knew exactly where I'd left the diagram.

Either that or I was going mad.

Next day I tried to talk to Hayley. If she really knew about Dad and was covering, I wanted to thank her. Also . . . well, I guess I just needed to tell *somebody* about Hermes and the Fuzzballs and everything.

Maybe she'd tell me I wasn't going mad.

Maybe those weren't the reasons.

When she dived firmly into her knot of friends at my approach and refused almost to look at me, I did something I had never done before. I had a fight. Trevor Heart was the name of the boy I fought. 'Big Trev', a year above me, a blunt-faced skinhead with a constant scowl. I'd been niggled by him a million times—everything about me from my colour down to the way that oxygen entered my lungs seemed to send him demented—but it was so easy to shut out that shit that he'd barely existed.

Today, for no reason, he did exist.

We were all in the lunch queue. He must have seen me trying to talk to Hayley, because he lumbered up to me from his place in the queue and said loudly, 'Got a bit o' skirt at last 'ave you, Jungle Bunny?' and I punched him on the ear.

For once, the first time maybe, the scowl lifted and a slow, ponderous smile inched painfully over his face. 'Outside then,' he croaked happily. So I followed him out to the playground with cries of '*fight fight fight*' following us.

As we rolled around on the cold tarmac with the sweet wrappers, tearing and hitting and grunting, Big Trev panted, 'That's more like it. Bloody girls, eh?' I thought, *You like this, do you, you mad bloody bastard?* and hit him again, much harder.

Then I went home.

I don't know whether Hayley was with the crowd watching the fight, but I had noticed the PE guy, Rose (*Mr* Rose) closing in fast. At this rate I wouldn't last at that place even until Dad was supposed to go in for the fictional interview.

Mrs Tanner, the weekly cleaner, was at our house today, which I'd forgotten. 'Not feeling too bright again, dear?' she asked.

Washing the blood from my face in the bathroom— the swelling round my eye was growing happily—I wondered if there were any negative conditions of body or mind for which she would not use that phrase.

'Not feeling too bright, are you, dear?' she would say one day to her drink-pickled, tar-encrusted husband as he was lowered into the ground.

When I came out and passed the doorway to the twins' room, she was in there, straightening the beds out, picking up toys. I watched as she absent-mindedly put both Karkos on Sophie's bed. Two identical Karkos sitting at the foot of Sophie's bed. Then one of the identical Karkos being picked up by Mrs Tanner's swollen, veiny hand and placed on the other (now re-made) bed.

'There,' she said. 'A nice cup of tea now, I think, before I do your father's room and yours.' Every pre-Mrs Tanner-night in a lamp-lit comedy I messed up Dad's bed—twirling the duvet round my head and then stepping all over it—and threw his clothes in the washing to keep her happy. Sometimes I brought in a little earth from the garden to rub into the carpet. 'You saw the card, I expect, dear? On the hall table.'

Those words went vaguely past in the background as I stared at the two ugly, lifeless Karkos. Their spiteful little claws digging into the bedding.

'Has he gone anywhere nice?'

'Who?' I asked, resurfacing stupidly.

'Your father, dear. A card from your father, I was saying. I suppose it's this new job of his, all that travelling? Very nice, too. Wouldn't mind a bit o' that myself.'

My guts contracted abruptly.

A card from Dad. Big deal. Whoopee-f**king-doo.

Mechanically, step by flaming meaningless step, I went downstairs again and stood in front of the hall table and looked at the card lying on top of it.

A round card, divided into six sections, each one with a picture. People holding up fish they'd caught, a beach in the bright sun, a beach at sunset with people in silhouette, a shot across tall buildings in some city, also in the bright sun, a chef cooking a big, spicy, fishy barbecue . . .

I felt sick. As usual, my head was throbbing. I went into the downstairs toilet and threw up.

On the other side of the card he'd written, in his tiny, exact writing, like mine:

Dear Julian,

I expect you are angry with me. Angry reading this. One day soon we will talk. I would like to phone you soon. Very soon.

To be honest, I don't really know what happened or why it happened. I have tried to be a good parent, but now I know that I have failed you. There are no excuses, only the apologies and regret of a man who felt suddenly that he was suffocating.

This will not be forever. Not even for long perhaps. I miss you, my family, very very much.

Take good care of the twins. You are a fine boy.

Dad.

PS   Are the systems working for you?

'Angry' didn't even come close. The white, scorching fury broke over me like a wave, blinding me, choking my senses. Not even a proper letter: just this crappy card. It crumpled and tore in my hands. Then I kicked the hall table to bits.

Mrs Tanner looked in round the door of the sitting room, where I had the horses on, a few minutes later. She looked frightened and unhappy.

'What *is* it, dear? What's wrong? You shouldn't go breaking things like that. It's not human. Not . . . civilized. Can I get you a nice cup of tea, eh, dear? How would that be?'

But there was nothing I could do to reassure the kind, interfering old lady. I was cut free from 'human' and 'civilized' and cups of tea.

'No,' I said. 'No thank you, Mrs Tanner. No tea.'

With frustration I could see that she was almost in tears. All these people on the edge of things, nothing to do with any of it, getting so upset.

'I'll be off now, then,' she said, wavering. I grunted

'OK' and she withdrew . . . but then her head poked back round and said: 'Your father, dear. He *is* all right, is he? It's just that I haven't really seen all that much of him. Not for a while.'

I made myself look directly at her, appearing neutral and relaxed. When the pressure was on I could do that; did it all the time at school. 'He's quite all right, Mrs Tanner. Just learning this new job. I think he left you a letter about that?'

Another forgery, left out for her with her money, weeks ago. Remembering it, she brightened up a bit.

'Yes, love. Yes, he did. Well, bye then.'

'Goodbye, Mrs Tanner.'

When she'd gone I wondered if she'd read that card herself. Almost certainly, I thought. Odds of at least 3 to 1 on. I'd have to think of something to keep the old gossip satisfied. Another one to add to the list. Liz and Mrs Sykes and the two schools and the pointing woman from the house across the road and now Mrs Tanner. But I didn't think Mrs Tanner was too bright . . .

Somewhere in the country the air was full of the sound of hooves on hard, frosted ground. The noise of the crowd was swelling as the bright parrot and canary silks came into view.

10

I think that Hayley didn't really believe me, about the stuff with Mr Hermes disappearing and his things all being stripped out of the place during school on Monday.

She asked, 'Isn't he the man you said crashed his car and seemed a bit drunk or something? The one who gave you the Spence.'

'Yeah.'

'Well, you said he was loopy.'

'So?'

'So he probably just decided to move and didn't tell anyone. Or maybe he was ill, like you said, and had to go into a home or hospital or something.'

I said patiently, 'And what about the break-in? What about the state inside the house? What about all the stuff going missing?'

Hayley had sensible answers for all of that. 'You don't *know* there was a break-in. Nothing was broken, was it? [No, it was a Yale lock: you wouldn't *need* to break it to get in.] Maybe this Mr Hermes just came back to get his computer and didn't shut the door properly. The mess doesn't mean anything: loads of people don't clean their homes properly. And if he was moving, I expect some big company came with a truck and cleared everything out. If he was ill, he'd hardly want to stagger around with all his furniture himself.'

Maybe I shouldn't have told her.

Maybe she was right, and old Hermes should save me a bed next to his in whatever loony bin he'd gone to.

I said weakly, 'What about the diagram I took, for Christ's sake?'

'You lost it?' she said brightly. 'Or maybe you thought you'd taken it but left it there by mistake?'

I was starting to accept her answers myself. I'd needed her to believe me. Seeing my face she took my hand and held it in both of hers.

'Of course,' she said gently, 'you might be right about everything. But if so, what's it all about?'

If I knew *that* . . .

Hayley probably had good reason for thinking I was a grade A nutcase, especially with what she'd found me doing when she came round. Digging a hole in the lawn.

After Mrs Tanner had gone, there'd still been no peace. I'd got so wound up that it'd felt like I would explode if I didn't talk to somebody.

I tried to go into the grey soup. Tried to let the horses work their magic. Dab Hand had actually bloody *won* on Monday: I could go out in a bit and collect my winnings, I thought; get some more bets down without having to use the worn cash card to fund them.

But it was no good. I wished Dad *had* called. Not being able to tell him what I thought of his card—what I thought of the whole flaming way he'd handled his life and his children—could easily have had me along the end of the road to borrow that crowbar that he had used before. I went out and walked endlessly round the garden, not able to keep a muscle in my body still.

In the morning I was the same and blew school away.

I rang Liz.

'Can I come today?'

'Yes, Julian. It's Wednesday. You're supposed to come today.'

Angry with myself for the slip, I went flat out to her place.

I think maybe I'd even been going to tell her. Everything: all about Dad and the twins and Hayley and the Fuzzballs. All that crap going round in my head until I thought I would go mental with it. But after the run there I was calmer, more focused again.

I talked to her instead about the chemical packets that biologists said contained our emotions.

I said, 'Why do you talk to people, nutters like me? Why not just do a blood test and hand out pills for whatever's missing in the brain. You know, pills for love or hunger or whatever's wrong?'

She said, 'You're not a *nutter*, Julian! [Of course I knew that!] And although it's true that some psychologists and people who study the brain and our feelings believe that eventually we will be able to do just what you suggest— produce drugs that can target emotional states very precisely—*I* think that it's better if we can heal ourselves, don't you? Talking to people can help us to understand and take control of our lives, which pills can't. But also it heals emotions. I mean, think about people crying their eyes out at *The Sound of Music* or laughing at some comedian describing how miserable he is in his marriage. We don't need pills to unlock these things.'

Without apparent connection, a rare sentence from Mum floated back to me. A time when I'd moaned in the launderette about being bored.

'Oho, bored are you?' she'd laughed, poking me under the ribs and tickling gently. 'Well, my poor, bored petal, think on this: we can but do the things we are given to do . . . with all our heart and mind and effort. This, my love, is how we make the beautiful shapes of life.'

It hadn't made much sense to the wriggling, scowling petal. Did we choose these things that we were 'given to do' or did *they* choose *us*? Still impossible to answer now. Were her statues magnetizing her? What about Dad and Self. He had put all his heart and mind and effort into destroying that almost-lovely thing. Dad had a dry, precise, detached sureness of what he would do in any situation. Was that worth more or less than Mum's passionate engagement with love, the elements, her stone . . . ?

If you let yourself go like that, feel so much, how could you be sure of anything?

I said to Liz, part of me squirming at playing the game, at doing what I was actually *there* for, 'Look, if there's stuff you want to say to somebody, but you *can't* . . . and the stuff is going round and round in your head . . . '

I tailed off.

She said, neutrally, 'Oh, that's an easy one. When that happens to me, I write it all down, in a letter. You know, a letter *to* that person. Say anything you want. Imagine the person receiving it and reading it and knowing how you feel. Except you don't have to post it, of course: you could just burn it or throw it away, or even bury it symbolically, if you felt like that.'

I thought about it and said, 'You are good at your job.'

And she said, teasingly, 'Maybe.'

There was no shame in just using things to help you

cope, ideas like that. After I'd run home I filled four sides of A4 with a letter to Dad and felt like death afterwards, drained of all blood or warmth. Liz hadn't said how painful that idea was. Also, I'd lost track of time, so the girls found me out the back with a spade, cutting out a neat square of turf from the place in the frozen ground where the silver tree had stood.

'What you doin', *Ju*-lian?' Sophie asked, interestedly.

'Burying a letter.' Ask a silly question.

'I think,' said Hayley, appearing behind them in the kitchen doorway, 'that Julian has lost his marbles and is looking to see if he has left them out here somewhere. Shall we help him look?'

My eyes met hers. Pale blue-grey. Laughing at me, but without cruelty.

Like I said, no wonder she thought I was nuts.

But afterwards, when the girls were in bed, she fussed about my bruises and rubbed cream into them, and the shudders she thought were just pain, were really my need for her.

'Thank you,' I said, feeling under her touch like a snake shedding its old skin, 'for lying to your mum.'

She kissed me and said, 'Tell me?'

So I told her, all about Dad and everything, even Mum. And at the end she didn't judge but just said, 'What are you going to do?'

I said, 'Try to keep social services and the rest away until I'm sixteen and then maybe they'll let me keep looking after the twins.'

'I can help a bit, maybe. With the twins and keeping Mum happy. Maybe you should know, though: your psychologist—Liz—was also asking about your dad and things when we were there.' She shot a glance at me sideways, slyly, very un-Hayley-like, I thought. 'I lied to her too.'

There was nothing I could do—Hayley was in the middle of it all, connected to all the parts of my life. I didn't know if I wanted to do anything about it, or not.

It was only much later that we got to the story of Hermes and the Fuzzballs. Maybe she didn't think that any of that was important compared to Dad leaving and trying to keep on top of everything. Maybe that's why she teased me and didn't really believe a word.

And like she said: what was it all about? A sick, middle-aged man, with a room full of newspaper clippings, and notes and documents, all about some kids' craze. Not exactly a heavyweight mystery.

She probably thought that compared to the two parcels of unpredictable, perfect life, by then asleep upstairs, nothing to do with Fuzzballs could be seen as having the tiniest significance.

With everything else I had to cope with, spending energy on *that* rubbish really was loony. Grade A.

11

Lucky Ferrin was going to get the Dome. The news had said he was the government's 'preferred bidder', which apparently meant he was in. A team of builders and designers and others, called 'our people' by the unsmiling giant, were brought over from America and were poised to move in and create *Fuzzball Futures*.

The giant said, 'We chose the name because we want our links with your great island to grow and solidify well into the future. *Our people* are just so excited to be over here, ready to make it all happen. Mr Ferrin can promise you . . . once your kids have seen what he will build here, their lives will be changed forever.'

Not giving the work to local people got Ferrin his first bad press, but in the Christmassy shops the great tinsel-covered Fuzzball stacks kept being eaten up and replaced in a never-ending surge for more. Barking mad. Psy-*chia*-trist mad.

Somewhere in the middle of all of it, a fit and healthy

and intelligent and kind middle-aged man had started selling the things, then gone mad or become obsessed or something, started living like an animal, then disappeared altogether, and his house was then raided, then stripped and sold.

When Hayley spoke I believed her doubts. Hearing her soft teasing voice, I thought that my grip on reality was slipping as much as Hermes's had done. The rest of the time I *knew* that some terrible thing was happening. Some big horror, right under our noses, brought over with 'our people'.

The best attempt I could make at re-doing the diagram of a molecule got only blank looks from the chemistry lot at school.

'You've got exams coming up after the Christmas break,' they said, switched like all flaming teachers just on to one little bit of life, one dead, dry, rotten bit. 'Stop wasting time and buckle down to some work. You need to impress a few people if you don't want to be in serious trouble.'

I could laugh in their faces about that. Exams. Serious trouble. None of them had a clue. Except that the trouble really *would* be serious when I got found out in the end and social services moved in. That stopped me from laughing all right. I was making too many mistakes . . .

A tiny, betraying *bastard* part of me whispered that if social services did come, I would be able to rest. When I thought that, I sweated it out on the streets or doing weights in the garden. I was so angry with myself: it was the kind of thing Dad would do. Just give in. Once I stuck a compass point part of the way into my hand, just to make that whisper disappear.

At least when I concentrated on finding out what Ferrin was up to and what they'd done to Mr Hermes it gave some kind of peace. Like with the horses. I tried ringing a few local hospitals and mental places—even the papers to ask about names in their 'Deaths' columns—but got nowhere, and just spent precious money that could be used to bet or buy food for us. All I really had now was the memory of my paper with its diagram, e-mail address, and the name, Dougie.

For the first time I visited the 'IT Centre' at school. The name was a joke: there were just two computers there, meant to encourage us to get into the ever-changing technology out of school hours or during study periods. Of course even with 'Squeaky' Michaels (another maths guy) putting his head in to keep an eye on things, most people were checking out porn and buying CDs or playing fantasy games with kids in Japan and Spain. It was easy to hide what they were doing with the warning noise his shoes made on the corridor lino. Probably, behind his vague, watery, washed-out blue eyes and grey moustache he knew pretty well what his equipment got used for, but was realistic enough not to make a fuss. Out of all of them I got to quite like him. He patiently showed me what I wanted to know and let me get on with it, not commenting that the IT Centre was suddenly a second home for me.

There were plenty of other nosy bastards, of course. The porn surfers and Lara fans couldn't accept me being there to start with. 'Come on, Egg, you prat, why don't you let somebody else use the sodding machine? You're not *doing* anything anyway!' But one way or another I got them to leave me alone on my pc, and the black-painted, windowless room with its perpetual computer hum was calming.

I went to lessons like a good boy. I had no more fights, no challenges to teachers. I even trained properly under Hewlett's nose, though I couldn't bring myself to care one way or the other about the area trials. Somehow sitting in front of the screen, chasing answers to the identity of that molecule, systematically trying different passwords to get into hermesk@aol.com, even logging on to the official Fuzzball website to see what I could learn there . . . all of that somehow got to be like the running had been, before.

But while I sat, calm and quiet, like a starship captain at the helm, destruction came closer and the forces gathered that would rip into our family and carry my sisters away from me.

I took to barring the front and back doors when I was at home, and keeping all the curtains and blinds shut, except for the twins' room. At night there was a self-designed sound alarm system inside the door: a stack of china and pans on a stool that would certainly wake me if it fell, whether the intruding enemy was 'our people' or social services or whoever. The Mrs Tanner problem was sorted with another forged letter: notice that her services weren't needed any more, plus a month's extra money to keep her happy. She hadn't mentioned Dad being away again, so everything was probably cool with her.

For the times I was with Hayley I had to put Fuzzballs out of my mind so that she thought I was being sensible, and also fight down the moods of panic and tension and anger that could rise up suddenly in my throat and frighten her away. She understood now why I was . . . under pressure: but I didn't want to test how much she'd put up with.

Oh, Christ, she was beautiful. When she left me I could often cry for her softness and gentle fun and understanding. But *with* her I had to be strong, funny, *something*.

I needed her. I didn't mind any more that she was a better parent to the twins than I was. She got closer as I drifted apart from them and felt all the connection with my sisters start to dissolve and melt. I was *stretched*, thin and taut like the skin on a drum. Even though I had nothing to give any more, nothing to do with love or joy, I was not going to let anybody touch us. That 'us' now included Hayley.

At night I was never properly asleep, always half listening for the falling china, and I think I could have killed in that state, if I heard the pile start to go.

Sessions with Liz got to be ultra-short. It wasn't the relaxed tea drinking and yoga shit, while I sprawled on the couch and easily twisted things round to suit me. Now it was a ten- or fifteen-minute live wire and I couldn't properly remember afterwards what we'd talked about, except that it was pain and maybe a bit of relief too and I was *angry* at her bloody self-righteous digging and thinking she knew every flaming thing about people.

A week before the time Dad was due to go into school I called again and managed to re-arrange the time for the meeting, put it back ten days. I said why not January, but the Head's secretary said that he wanted to get it sorted before Christmas. I realized that eventually—soon—a day would come when my father was 100 per cent expected either at my school or the twins', and he wouldn't be there, and then their bloody alarm bells would ring and something would happen.

Something. The flaming end.

Even if I thought of a way out (I wondered if I could hire someone, an actor or someone, to go in and pretend to be Dad) there was another threat waiting to blow the starship apart.

I don't even know how it happened. Putting the cash card into the machine one day to get money for some bets, I saw the balance and it was less than £500. I called the bank, got a statement sent, but it was right. The money was almost gone.

And I didn't know enough yet. I had to have more practice before I could make my own system. I was so *close* to blowing the whole thing wide open, understanding how the races worked, making a flaming *mint*. It just wasn't fair.

Of course the betting was another thing I had to try and keep from Hayley: or at least the amount of betting. I thought I would go mad, so many things to be careful about, so many things that different people mustn't know. I was the spider at the centre of the web, feeling the twitching of all the different strands, having to build and repair and deal with every last threat. I was as twitchy as the spider, never sleeping.

Also, at the centre of the Web. (The World Wide one.) Sitting in the calm darkness in every minute that someone didn't actually need me somewhere else, my fingers caressing the small squares that could get me flying anywhere. Sooner or later, I thought, I would get what I wanted. Someone would give me answers on the scanned molecule-attempt that I was sending out. Someone would know Dougie. Someone would know *something*. In the meantime it was a way to stay away from the horses: a smooth, efficient, ordered relief from the surge of excitement that the bets could bring. (With less than £500 left I was trying to limit myself to total bets of no more than £50 a week. Maybe, just maybe, it would be enough to complete my knowledge.)

When I did finally get what I wanted, the same betting surge was there—as if my horse had won by a head—but with it came disappointment. Who needed bloody answers? Who cared what Ferrin was doing, or about Hermes? I could stay in the IT Centre for ever.

It was <u>hermesk@aol.com</u> that got me there. In between all the different screens I had up—science chatrooms, scrolling lines of results given by search engines to my questions, e-mail directories containing 'Dougie'—I was idly tapping possible passwords for Hermes's mailbox . . .

and after a hundred wrong attempts, got it right. Just like that.

'Spence'.

Flaming obvious.

But 'Spence' with Hermes's house number tagged on the end, making 'Spence47'.

Magically, without warning, the screen blossomed and said:

Welcome back Kostas Hermes. You have 31 new messages.

I was *in*!

Nobody had been inside that mailbox for a long time, not for five weeks or so. Most of the e-mails were nothing. MSN offering free downloads of their virtual-monopolies. Junk mail. Something that seemed to be from some old relative of Hermes, living in the States. Dull, work-related messages: revised sales targets, new Fuzzball products that Hermes would be expected to handle. He couldn't have had a difficult job, I thought, since the shops and the kids wanted any Fuzzball crap they could get their hands on. My eyes ran down the total in-box list and found what I wanted straight away: a message from Dougie.

It wasn't the mail where he'd sent the molecule, which was what I'd really wanted. (That one didn't seem to be here.) It just said:

I'm going on two weeks leave tomorrow. Some sun at last. I don't expect we'll be talking again. Good luck.

Dougie

God knows what I'm going to do when I get back.

One of the Lara freaks, a Pakistani kid called Khan, ambled up and looked over my shoulder. 'Piss off,' I said, and he went. OK, so there was no molecule, but there was a chance that I could now speak to Dougie, the molecule sender, the guy who *must* know what was going on. With a racing pulse I clicked on the 'reply' button on the screen and then sat thinking, while the cursor blinked away in the top, left-hand corner. I wondered if what I was doing was legal, and also thought about the chance that Hayley was right and that there *was* no mystery. Dougie would think I was nuts.

OK, I was into Hermes's box so the answer was to write *as* the sad old git himself. I typed:

Dear Dougie,

I know you said we wouldn't be in contact again, but I have some problems. Can we talk? Can I ask you some things?

E-mail me back to this box please.

Then I clicked on 'add signature' and the machine added:

Best Wishes

Kostas Hermes

One more pause before clicking on 'send'. Then the thing was done and I was committed. Or should be.

No answer came for three days. In that time I fell suddenly into black, hopeless, depression; found myself putting on spread bets worth £82 between them; missed half an afternoon of school to watch the horses lose almost all of my money; and pretended to be ill so Hayley wouldn't come round.

My weakness made me hate myself. So many failures that I could avoid with just the smallest bit of effort. It was pathetic. It made me understand how Dad had been angry enough to smash Self. Why couldn't Mum have made it right? Why make it ugly when you could make it beautiful and whole with just that small effort.

We were all insects in my family. Failures, except for the twins, and out of everything my being a failure to them made me most angry. Out of all the despairing, sometimes tearful resolutions made during the long sleepless nights, the resolution to get my flaming act together for *them* was the strongest. I *wouldn't* do it again, *wouldn't* fail, *wouldn't* bet, *wouldn't* get angry, *wouldn't* . . .

. . . but it was no good. I was a shit.

Maybe Sophie and Tanya would turn into insect failures too, after all. Maybe it was in the Egg genes. When I did their homework with them, I saw in their books their teacher's comments about presentation and effort.

Do use a ruler, Sophie!

Write on the line, please. Do this again at home.

Try to take more care.

And lots more of that kind of rubbish.

'You're not trying very hard, are you?' I said to them. 'Look at the work you did at the beginning of term. Here, at the start of your books. That was lovely work, wasn't it? Look at how neatly you did these words here . . . and these nice pictures with all the different colours . . . '

They obediently made their eyes follow what I was showing them from the first pages of their exercise books. But those eyes were glazed, unreachable, resentful, totally bored.

'So do we have to do this again or can we go an' play?'

They were already getting up. Instinctively I caught an arm—Tanya's arm—to stop the flight. She looked round, down at where my hand held her. She tried to pull away.

'You're hurtin' me, *Ju*-lian.'

I let go.

'OK. OK, go and play. We'll eat in half an hour.'

I couldn't force them to make an effort, could I? Even with their reading, their favourite thing from school, they were going backwards. I bought new books in case they were bored with the other ones, and they got left unread on the floor.

I was losing all my battles.

With no more need to research for the moment, I still ended back in the IT room. Back in the calming darkness. Restlessly, I just played with the machines, looked at betting and racing sites for a bit, and eventually—with the jeering encouragement of the rest of the nothings in there—ended up as one of the porn surfers. Even in this sanctuary I brought my own failure with me and ruined the peace I'd found. The screen pictures excited and fascinated me and swamped me with guilt. When I did see Hayley I could hardly meet her eye. I wanted *her*, not the other. The two things were poles apart, and I was lost.

Then, checking Hermes's box for the millionth time, it was there. A reply.

It just said:

Today. 5pm. IRC Undernet. #Chatzone. I'll find you.

I called Khan over and showed him. 'What's IRC? What's Undernet?'

He said, 'IRC is Internet Relay Chat. Undernet is one of the IRC networks. These machines don't have IRC, but you could download the software before five. Who is this guy, anyway? What are you up to, Egg, you f**king weirdo?'

'Just show me the download,' I said, 'and then shut up.'

Khan was OK. At 5p.m. I'd equipped the machine with the right software downloads, missing more lessons to do it, and was waiting in #Chatzone, a huge 'room' with perhaps 500 people or more in it.

At 5.01 he arrived.

Incoming DCC from 'Duntocher'. Will you accept DCC?

I clicked on 'Accept'.

Duntocher: What's going on? I can give you two minutes.

Hermes: How was your leave?

Duntocher: F**k that. F**k the leave. We weren't supposed to be in further contact.

Hermes: OK, sorry, but I lost the diagram. Can you e-mail it again?

Duntocher: I don't have it. I told you it was a one-off. LOST IT? You crazy Greek idiot.

Hermes: Well, what else can you tell me, then? About the Fuzzballs. Anything will help. Or about the molecule.

Long pause

Duntocher: Who are you? Where's Hermes?

Hermes: Hermes has disappeared. I'm just . . . a friend. I want to help.

Duntocher: Forget it. Whoever you are, forget EVERYTHING. Just . . .

Then something else happened: without warning the DCC screen flicked off and another took its place. No offered choice this time of whether to accept the link or not. No nickname either: just a couple of lines of text.

Our friend's advice is good. Forget everything. We have monitored your transmission. We have your IP number. We know who you are. Forget everything.

I'd barely read the message when the screen blinked away, along with all the screens behind it. In fact, the computer just crashed. The screen went black and the fan motor trailed off. I was sitting in front of a dead machine.

I sat unmoving for a while, then rubbed my eyes and looked at my watch. It was 5.35. How could that be? The conversation with Dougie had only lasted a minute or two. With my head swimming I left the IT Centre. Someone in there called after me:

'Hey, man! Hey, you crazy Egg! What have you done to that 'puter? HEY!'

I didn't listen. I was late for the twins. I was shaking. Letting myself out of the school gates, I jogged home on legs like jelly.

12

Other gaps started appearing in my day-to-day life. Bits of time lost like in the IT place. For the first time I wondered if I *was* in fact mad. Properly mad. Maybe something in my genes from my kooky mum in her snowstorm of stone dust and my loser dad who couldn't keep her, couldn't even keep his children, just chickened out of everything.

Khan told me that Michaels was looking for me about that machine, wanting some kind of explanation. On the mat at home a deluge of unwelcome mail rained down. A dinner invitation to the whole family from Mrs Sykes, RSVP. A reminder from the two school secretaries of Dad's appointments, only a few days away now. A clutch of bills that I had barely enough money to pay. The confirmation of my entrance to the area cross-country trials, also only days away, with a fee payable of £8. And a card from Hayley, a neat shiny silver square with a tiny red heart in the centre. She'd written:

Please don't be distant. I can't bear it. I miss you. Love, Hx

Tanya, peeping round my shoulder, puzzling out the words, said, 'What's *dis-tant*?'

I looked at her, saw a sad little girl, cradling her Karko close and sucking her thumb. I realized that she was in a state: she needed her hair brushing out properly, needed her school clothes washing and ironing. It was a shock, because I was good at that, on top of it all.

I said, 'It means she wants to see more of me.'

Tanya said, copying my phrase, 'Yes, *we* want to see more of each other.' I didn't know what she meant: the twins and Hayley? The twins and me? Just the twins?

I needed Hayley. That closeness coming back from Uttoxeter, the dozing on the train, felt like a hundred years ago instead of last month. Why couldn't she understand that I pushed her away in case I ruined everything and in case *she* out of all of them thought I was mad.

I went to Liz and with gut-wrenching difficulty said to her, 'I don't feel I'm coping.'

She said, 'No,' and waited expectantly.

I told her all about the Fuzzballs, everything from Hermes crashing his car to the computer message. I showed her the attempted copy of the molecule. I told her about the stack of china inside the door and the snooker cue by my bed.

She didn't laugh, but held the paper and said in her neutral way, 'What about the police?'

What about social services?

I said, 'What could I tell them? I have no evidence. Not a single thing but my memory. They'd think I was nuts, wouldn't they?'

'Possibly. What does your father think?'

Trying to match the neutral tone—*was* it neutral? Had she tensed up a bit while she waited for the reply?—I said, 'Not much. He's not interested.'

'OK, so apart from this mystery and your feeling that someone is possibly watching you or might break in and harm you and your sisters, how do you feel generally? Tell me about your state of mind. Tell me about school, or home. Whatever.'

How much could I tell her?

I looked at the ridged pattern of material along the arm of the couch, ran my fingers over it, first against the ridges, then along them.

'Like I said, I don't feel I'm coping. I feel . . . under pressure. I feel, no, I *know*, that lots of those . . . people . . . in my life are trying to trip me up, or wanting more than I can give. I feel *drained*.'

She said nothing, didn't poke at me with words or questions. It was called 'creating a safe space' or something: she'd told me about it once, when she'd explained what psychologists did. And now I'd started, drawn into the 'safe space' like a real nutcase, I couldn't flaming stop. Babbling like a child. All about Hewlett and Mrs Sykes and Shah and Hayley and Big Trev. About Dad having to go into school to discuss my future. About the twins being in trouble, getting so *wild*. Even about the betting, the relief that I'd got from the IT room, the bits of time—five or ten minutes here and there—that I'd started to 'lose'.

Liz stayed quiet while I spilled it all out. Everything except the fact that Dad had gone. I wasn't an idiot.

When I'd finished the room was in shadows, the light going. She left it like that a minute or two and then went and switched on some lamps, but nothing blinding.

Then she said, 'You obviously feel that people are asking too much of you. That you have too much responsibility.'

'Yes.'

'So why don't we work on you being kind to yourself for a while.'

I didn't understand what she meant.

'Instead of looking at the ways you're failing, or that you *believe* people see you as failing, let's focus on the ways you're succeeding. All the many, many wonderful, positive things about *you*, Julian Egg. Your loving devotion to your sisters, the fact that a person like Hayley likes you very much, your abilities in maths and sport, your basic kindness . . .'

'*Kindness?* You're mad yourself, Liz.'

'No, it's there. Believe me. You *care*, Julian. But . . . *but*—and this is the $64,000 part now—if you can't be good to yourself, love *yourself*, how can you possibly be kind to other people?'

Oh, brother. Like something from the God channel or something. I guess my face showed what I thought, but Liz carried on:

'You can't draw water out of the well if you don't allow new rain to fill it again. My advice to you, for the next week, is this. Don't care what other people's expectations of you are. Just do the best that *you* feel you can do. And love yourself for that. Look at all the ways you are succeeding. Only take on responsibilities if you really want them and are comfortable with them. Let your father worry about the bigger things. Just be the best person that *you* can be and don't mind what the rest think.'

My head swam with it all. How did Liz's 'love yourself' fit in with Mum's, *We can but do the things we are given to do . . . with all our heart and mind and effort*? Was it the same? Was this, my love, how we made the beautiful shapes of life?

It was all probably just kooky shit. Again my brain said that Dad was right to choose the dried beans, something certain you could depend on.

Frustrated, weak from too much talking nonsense, I said, 'So what about the Fuzzballs stuff? What about Mr Hermes disappearing? What about that molecule?'

'Well . . . ' she looked doubtful. 'Leave the diagram with me and I'll ask a chemist friend if you like. But maybe you should forget about the Fuzzballs too, for a while.'

Great. 'And what if somebody, Ferrin or somebody, decides to come and get me? Or to harm my family?'

She said carefully, 'Julian, it *is* possible, the way you are feeling now, that things like that can seem bigger—or more important—than they really are. You know, you're under pressure, so there are phantoms everywhere.'

OK. Liz didn't believe me either. I got up to leave.

'I'd like you to see someone else, though. A doctor. For those dizzy spells, just to be certain. A quick check-up.'

I said, 'OK, I will.' And left.

Talking about it hadn't helped. The nuclear disaster of our family got nearer and nearer. Whatever Ferrin was up to, I was alone and couldn't touch him. Maybe it was true, anyway, that I was imagining it.

I tried, really tried, to forget every bad thing. I tried to love myself, reminded myself of everything I could do, all the good stuff about Julian Egg. I had Hayley round again. She knew that disaster was coming but thought it was for the best now.

'The people from social services are only going to want to look after you. They're not monsters, are they? You won't have to worry about money any more. There'll be someone to help you with the twins.'

I said, 'What about my family? It won't bloody exist any more, will it? What business is it of theirs anyway?'

And she held me and whispered, 'Sweet Jules. Poor love.' Thin, white-faced Hayley comforting *me*. I hated my weakness. Hated how I needed her.

On telly, the news man said, 'The government confirmed today that the Millennium Dome site in east London has been sold to a consortium headed by Fuzzball billionaire Lucky Ferrin, for an as-yet undisclosed sum. Issuing a statement from the UK Fuzzball production headquarters at Duntocher, near Glasgow, Mr Ferrin said that he was "pleased and satisfied" with the deal. He promised that the planned Fuzzball Futures would change the face of London forever.'

!!!

I wasn't sure whether I could make it up to Glasgow and back in a day, so I took the twins. With the new information my mind clicked smoothly into gear, like when I'd been woken by the break-in, and I reckoned my sisters would be safer with me than without me, even going there. Not that anything was safe, for us. Not now.

Hayley said *no way* was she coming, not after last time and getting grounded by her mum. 'What are you going there for, Jules? What can you hope to find? It's just a factory. You're not being fair to the girls, dragging them all the way up there.'

She did come too, though, as I'd expected: appeared on the station platform in the cold dark morning, with a closed-up face.

'You nut,' she said fiercely, 'I'm only coming for them.'

'I know.' I kissed her. 'Thank you.'

'You'll have to pay for my ticket too.'

All the rest of Dad's money was in my pocket, drawn out the day before. It didn't matter any more anyway, none of it did. I could always sell stuff from the house if I needed cash: but with Armageddon only three or four days away, there was no point leaving anything in the account. Social services were bound to stop Dad's card when they moved in. Anyway, maybe we just wouldn't go back home. Maybe I'd take the twins somewhere else, get a job . . .

For the moment I was going to nail Ferrin. That was the main thing. Somehow I felt that bastard was behind all the bad stuff that had happened to us. Him and Dad, of course. In my dreams I could hardly tell them apart.

The twins were bright-eyed, excited, and hopping around to have a change in the routine. They grabbed Hayley's coat sleeves and held on tight. Remembering how good it had been last time, to get away, I knew how they felt. In the steamed-up, sour-smelling train I unpacked the bag of games I'd brought. Cards, ludo, snakes-and-ladders, colouring books. Also crisps, chocolate, hard-boiled eggs, tomatoes, olives, bread and honey, drinks. Loads of stuff. We wouldn't suffer.

Even so, after the first three hours, surrounded now by wrappers and stickyness and egg shell and tomato seeds, Tanya and Sophie thought it was time to stop being on a train and do something different.

'We nearly there, *Ju*-lian?' they asked.

'Nearly,' I lied.

Hayley sat opposite me, studying my face. She looked sad. I seemed to be surrounded by people who looked like that these days. I tried a smile but she just went on looking at me in the same way. Then sort-of shrug-shuddered, and turned to point something out to the girls, a river or something that we were passing. Later on I read a story aloud, *Five Minutes' Peace*, about Mrs Bear trying to get personal space away from her kids.

'Just like you,' Sophie yawned. Then they were away, sleeping, and we stayed quiet until the train groaned in to the station at Glasgow.

The problem was: even if the twins were safer staying with me at the moment, would that still be true if I took them to the Fuzzball factory? With Hayley there, I'd thought she could take them to a park or ice-skating or whatever there was to do in this place, while I went and had a look. Alone I might well get inside: there were pliers and screwdrivers and a hacksaw in my little rucksack. If it turned out it was worth staying longer I could come back and find them and we could sort out a place to sleep. I hadn't paid those bills at home, so I reckoned the money in my pocket would be OK, for now. (How much did it cost, to stay in a B and B, I wondered.)

Hayley had other ideas.

'No way, Jules. No way are you bringing us all the way up here and dumping us while you go off and do your loony stuff. Really. I've almost had it with you. We're bloody coming too. And then later, we're getting the train back again. There's a late one we can catch just before seven. I'll phone Mum to say I'm going to stay at yours tonight. She thinks you're all coming to supper this week anyway, so maybe she won't mind. It's school tomorrow, though. We're not staying here.'

It was a shock to hear her swear and say that, that she'd 'almost had it' with me. Why did she feel like that? What had I done, for Christ's sake? I wanted to say, *OK, if that's how you feel, then you can just . . .*

I said instead, 'Let's find a bus then.'

Everything that had to be worked out—including Hayley and me—could wait until I'd got something on Ferrin.

We got a bus and some strange looks. 'You *do* go that far, do you?' I asked the driver. 'Out to Duntocher?' (It was pronounced Dun-toke-er, and I'd found it on the map before coming, a small outer-suburb at the western edge of the city, next to the River Clyde and a bridge called the Erskine Bridge.)

The driver said, 'Och aye: that's what it says on the front. I go there, right enough.' But he still looked at us like we were aliens. We sat down at the back, the twins started to ask about when we were going to eat again, Hayley told them soon, don't worry, and I watched the winter streets of Glasgow and Clydebank slowly grind by. Soon there was a blanket of grey rain coursing down the window, to match the dark heavy skies. I could see why the driver had looked at us like that, could see why we didn't fit in here. The only thing I had to do now, though, was stay focused. See the thing through. Like racing from the front.

At Duntocher, which seemed a bleak, grey place nestling at the bottom of a small hillside, swept by wind and rain coming in along the river from the sea, I asked somebody about the factory and he pointed at the corner of a black, flat-roofed building that was just visible round the shoulder of the hill, and said, 'Up there.'

'Bloody hell, Jules,' Hayley said wearily. There was no love in the way she looked at me. It wasn't like the races, this time, after all.

We found a road and trudged up towards our target. The twins, (thankfully) kitted out in their wellies, half-heartedly jumped in puddles and complained of hunger, thirst, boredom . . . When we finally struggled round a corner and found it, a gleaming, opaque black cube, tucked away behind electric fences that were topped by CCTV cameras, I could have sat down and cried. My pathetic collection of tools! No way could anyone get in here.

Stay focused.

'Come on,' I said, and led them up the private road to the front gate. There wasn't even a plaque or notice saying what the factory was. Maybe, I thought, the gate man would know Dougie. Maybe he lived near here. Sooner or later we had to get a break. Didn't we? I wished I knew Dougie's surname.

Next to the entrance—not, as I'd imagined, a single wooden arm that swung up and down to let things past, but high and, according to a notice, also electrified, double gates—was a metal cubicle, a place for the man on sentry duty to sit, with all the controls. There were two men in there at the moment, one in a security uniform and another one, and when I rang the buzzer on our side of the fence and waved, it was not the security man that came out.

'Good afternoon. Can I help you?'

Dressed in a suit, holding a smart black umbrella, certainly holding no trace of Scottish accent, he reminded me of someone. With sudden nausea, I thought for a moment that it was the so-called estate agent I'd found in Hermes's place. He had the same dark eyes and hair, the same compact look. I forced myself into calmness. No, not the same man: similar, but there *were* little differences.

I sensed Hayley looking at me questioningly as if to say: *Well? We've come all the way up here on your wild goose chase. What now? Are we just going to walk away?*

I floundered and said, 'Err, we just came to have a look. My sisters are Fuzzball crazy and so . . . ' It sounded pretty pathetic. Maybe this wasn't even the right place after all.

' . . . and so,' the man finished smoothly for me, 'you'd like to see inside? See how they're made? Something to tell your friends, at school? Well . . . I think that would be OK, just this once. I've got a spare hour, so let me show you round.'

He signalled to the uniform man to buzz the big electric gates open wide for us and in a dream I led the way though, into Ferrin's world.

It was almost completely automated. Apart from the man with us and the gate man we saw only three other people there: two security guards with Rottweilers, endlessly patrolling the plant, and one man in a control centre, high up and overlooking the gleaming, never-still production line that wove across the factory floor below. This man had banks of lights and buttons to monitor, and was reading the *Sun* when we entered.

Our guide said, 'We have some guests: please welcome them. They are fans, apparently.'

The control man quickly shoved the paper away under his chair and looked nervous, even afraid, although he didn't seem to have been told off that I could see. He shook our hands, even the twins' (which made them giggle) and said, 'Yes, er, welcome to the plant. We're very . . . er . . . proud.' His glance flicked across to our guide all through this welcome, like a child who didn't know yet how angry it had made its dad. Would it just be bed with no tea, or a real beating?

Apart from reading the paper, he didn't seem to have much to worry about. Maybe he was just crazy.

All six of us went down to the factory floor—'You may address any technical queries to my colleague here,' said our dark-suited guide—and the twins were in instant heaven. For them, at least, the long, long trip had suddenly become worthwhile. Hundreds upon hundreds of Fuzzballs of every possible colour and shape were on the move round the plant. Some with fur, some with feathers, some as bald as stones, some sinister, some cuddly-cute, some armed with claws and teeth like the Karkos that I'd insisted were left at home for the day. We wandered round and watched them being dyed and having their eyes put in and the 'Special Abilities' labels being automatically attached round their necks. We even saw them being boxed and then trundling in automatic carts on rails to be stacked in the back of two huge trucks that stood in a loading bay.

No sign of any drivers.

'How many?' I asked the nervous man. 'How many a day?'

He glanced almost imperceptibly at Dark-Suit (did *he* give a tiny nod?) before replying. 'Approaching ten thousand. We're very efficient.'

Ten thousand a day, just in Britain, and the shops were selling out daily. I saw the twins in a happy trance, just staring at the lines of Fuzzballs, more contented than they'd been all day.

Hayley said, 'I feel a bit sick.'

Our guide said, 'It's probably the dyes. It often takes people like that, if you're not used to it.' Then, to his colleague, 'Please take our charming young visitor and show her the facilities.'

Hayley smiled gratefully at him and went. I wanted to punch his lights out, but felt quite dizzy myself. There was something hypnotic about the never-ceasing machinery.

Keep focused, I thought. Several times I tried to leave the group and wander around alone but never managed it, and Dark-Suit said, 'Better to stay together. Most of the machinery is unfenced as there is so little need for personnel. We really couldn't afford an insurance claim.'

He made it sound like a joke, but I could hear an order underneath. Dark-Suit was used to people—the nervous, *Sun*-reading controller for one—doing what he said. I stayed with the others, but looked round intently to find something out of place, something sinister, something to do with a chemical molecule. But that could be anything. Everything in the universe was made of flaming chemicals. And the molecule might just be something illegal that Ferrin was up to, behind the front of the Fuzzballs business.

Alone, with a few hours, maybe I could have found something. Christ knows what. But *this* . . . this faceless plant didn't give me a chance. I'd expected people, workers I could talk to as they left at the end of the day, cleaners even, perhaps the chance to have a poke around when everything was locked up. *This* place wouldn't stop, I thought: the machines would keep turning smoothly all night. The electricity would fizz through those fences, the cameras would swivel, full trucks would be driven away by unknown drivers and replaced by empty vehicles. The control man would probably be replaced at night by another, doing the same monitoring job.

Faceless and inhuman. Hypnotic.

It was hard to think.

Hayley was back and to the twins' delight, Dark-Suit now took us to the loading area and offered them their choice of a new Fuzzball each. Sophie took one of the rock-looking ones, squat and grinning; Tanya hesitated and then took something that looked like a caterpillar, its eyes hidden by great bushy brows.

'What about you two?' Dark-Suit asked me and Hayley. 'Come on now, there are no age limits on our little friends. Fun for everyone, the whole family. What about one for our delightful young lady, at least?'

Hayley started to say something, but I spoke quickly, brusquely, 'No, not for either of us, thank you. We're fine.'

Dark-Suit flashed me a split-second, angry-looking glance—again that impression of steel and thunder underneath, making his black eyes even blacker—and then was all smiles again.

'Of course,' he said. 'As you wish. In that case, let me escort you back to the gate. I'm afraid I shall have to return to my other duties now.'

And that was it, we found ourselves out in the rain

again, blinking in the dim afternoon, walking back to the gate. A flaming useless waste of time.

At the metal cubicle, the gate man was watching us and held out a phone to Dark-Suit. 'The chief for you, sir,' he said in a heavy Scottish accent. Dark-Suit took the phone and said, 'Open the gate for our visitors. I'll just be a moment.' And then into the mouthpiece: 'Yes, sir?'

The gate man pressed his buttons to set the electric barrier silently swinging inwards. He was old and wheezed as he leaned over the controls. We were huddled outside, since the open-sided cubicle couldn't have held all of us. I took the girls' hands and started walking through the now-open gate and, as I'd hoped, the gate man came out and wheezed after us.

'The boss'll want to say goodbye, I'm thinking. Why don' youse just wait back there?'

Dark-Suit was watching through the glass, but still listening to whoever was speaking on the phone, the Chief. We were too far away to hear him, and vice versa. I said to the gate man, 'Do you know Dougie? He works here sometimes.'

I didn't *know* whether he worked there or not, but there was no time to think clearly. My brain was still reeling from being inside the airless, windowless black cube.

The old man wasn't as well trained as the other one we'd met, inside. Or maybe he was just old and forgetful. He said, 'Dougie? Och no, he's . . .'

'He's what?'

'Well, hope youse all had a good visit,' he mumbled.

Dark-Suit had joined us and stood at my elbow. The gate man wheezed back to his post, looking paler, I thought.

There was no mistaking the thunder in our guide's face now. His voice hardly changed, though. 'Thank you for

121

coming,' he said in his slippery, posh voice. 'I do hope you have a good trip down south.'

Then the hours and hours of journey, the same as the morning, but in reverse.

Grey bus through grey rainy Glasgow and then stinking train grinding down south.

The twins ate sandwiches from the buffet, sat cuddling their new Fuzzballs in sleepy silence and eventually lay across the seats.

'Thank you, Jules, for the lovely day,' Sophie murmured, before slipping into sleep.

Hayley was also quiet.

'That man!' I said. 'He knew where we came from. He knew who we were. He said to have a good trip *down south*.'

Hayley said, 'For heaven's sake. It wasn't hard for him to guess, was it? That we don't live in Glasgow. Grow up, Julian.'

Little, white-faced shy Hayley.

Eventually she slept too, and at least leant against me.

The most I could hope for.

13

I don't know how it happened, but that week I completely lost it. No, I didn't go mad. I ran away.

It was the second week of December. The week of the area trials, the week of Dad's interviews with the two school headteachers, the week of a family dinner with Mrs Sykes (RSVP), and the week the money would run out.

Those ten thousand Fuzzballs a day poured down over the border and drowned the country. In London, work started on Fuzzball Futures. Ferrin and Dark-Suit and his brother the 'estate agent' were winning. They'd known all about the trip to Duntocher: that guy had been *waiting* for us specially. The gate man had known who I meant by 'Dougie' and he'd been silenced.

I couldn't be bothered with going into school. There didn't seem much point any longer. I sat at home watching TV, put a few small bets on, walked around the shops unable to settle. Seeing the decorations and stuff I thought that I should be doing that at home, should be making the place seem like Christmas for the twins, even if we weren't going to be there. So I nipped back and got a suitcase and a rucksack and filled them with stuff of Dad's and my CD player and the posh clock from the mantelpiece—loads of rubbish that didn't make any difference to your life, not really—and sold it all to a second-hand shop. The whole lot, suitcase and rucksack included, got me £135, enough for a Christmas of some sort. The TV would be next, I thought, but the twins wouldn't thank me for that. I'd have found a way to shift the car if it hadn't disappeared with Dad.

Before putting up any decorations I made a real effort and cleaned the whole flaming house. It needed it, since Mrs Tanner had stopped coming. Four hours dusty slog that made me sweat more than a race.

Sometimes I was crying. Crying without even noticing, then suddenly feeling the wet or catching sight of my face in the mirror. What a *nothing*, I thought. What a spineless *failure*.

Hewlett rang and said, grimly, 'You seem to be heading for meltdown, at school. Nobody sees you much now, I understand. And there was some business about a computer. You *are* going to be there for the race this week, I take it?'

'Yes.'

'Well, see that you are, Egg, or I'll come and find you myself.'

We were supposed to be driving down there in his messy old Rover, stinking of dog and mints and rotten leather. Two flaming hours, each way. It didn't matter, nothing did, but the thought made me feel sick. I wanted to ask Hayley to come too, but I knew she wouldn't want to see me any more. Everything was finished.

When Hewlett had rung off, the phone went again, almost before it was in its cradle.

'Hello?' I said. I thought Hewlett wanted to say something else; make some other threat maybe, about not being late. *See that you're there on time, Egg, or we'll find you a part in the school play next week.*

' . . . Julian?'

Dad.

I saw pure white, stabbed in blindness for the button to silence him, crashed the phone down into its holder, sat back heavily on the bottom step of the stairs.

The phone rang again and after five rings the answer machine clicked in. Still seeing nothing, I sat hugging my knees while his voice spewed out of the speaker. He was missing us. He had got some work. The weather was hot. There was some woman he'd met. He loved us. Maybe he would be back soon. Maybe in a month or two. It wasn't as good as he'd thought. He hated himself for what he'd done.

Liar. It was all lies. All weakness and apology and as ugly as Self.

I wanted to pick the phone up again and say, 'Stay there. Don't come back. Disappear,' . . . but I couldn't move.

I was still there when the girls arrived.

'OOOOHHH,' they said. 'Chris'mas! We gonna have a tree too? What you getting us? Is *Hay*-ley coming?'

They came and sat on the stairs with me.

Sophie said to Tanya, like I wasn't there, '*Ju*-lian's sad. *We* gotta look after him, like he looks after us.'

Tanya said, 'We can make pizzas an' he can help.' And then, gently, to me, 'You can choose your things to go on top: *anything*, like us.'

'No rotten ol' olives,' whispered Sophie.

I got a tree and then blew the rest of the cash that I'd got from selling our stuff. £90, on a horse called Last Chance, all dark and shining and muscly and looking directly out at me from the TV, saying: *Choose me. I know this game. I have only fooled them into giving me these odds of 20 to 1. Look at my condition. This is my day. Nobody can stop me.* The buzz was great, down at the betting shop. The first big bet I'd placed for ages.

Afterwards, before I'd even got home, the inevitable hot, hopeless shame filled me, so that I didn't bother to watch the race.

On Wednesday the doggy Rover bounced into the carpark field after two silent, numb hours, and Hewlett said, 'Go on then, lad. Get warmed up. You've got precisely fifteen minutes until the start time for your class. I've got to go and confirm entry and get a number for you.' He strolled off, lighting his pipe, greeting other teachers and people he knew.

It wasn't even my fault that we were late. His wife was ill, apparently. Either that or he was just late and needed an easy excuse. He didn't seem very worried. After all that crap, too, about me turning up on time.

This is the last one, I thought, *the last race for you, Hewlett. Then you can find another pillock to kill himself in the cold and rain.*

The area trials were set in a large sweep of empty, undulating countryside with a biting wind blowing the long, straggly grass flat and occasional thorny bushes punctuating what fences there were: all barbed wire. It was how I imagined the Russian Steppes or those miles of nothing in Siberia or Mongolia or wherever it was. An empty, drab land even with a thousand runners, markers, watchers, and officials messing about in it.

For ten minutes I stretched and jog-sprinted across the churned-up carpark field. Then, feeling sick as usual, I pinned on the number Hewlett had brought me, and went down to the start. Forty or so runners of my age were lined up in their trendy Nikes and technical fabric vests. This, my love, is how we make the beautiful shapes of life. Oh, Christ.

The gun went.

Choosing to put everything that wasn't running on a distant star in an imploding universe, I fought for space in the pack and focused on the first marking point, easily visible over half a mile of that grass wasteland.

I had never done anything that hurt so much, physically. But what was physical pain? Physical pain was unimportant: a relief even, blowing away the clogged dust and slime of fear and guilt that never left me now. I would walk on hot coals not to see the sadness in my sisters, the coldness in Hayley.

The run-from-the-front Julian Egg wouldn't have made it: he'd have been squashed early on, but the shapes and the chemical streams of my life were changing now. I ran until the pain in my lungs and heart and belly filled my universe.

The course was two circuits of a three-mile loop, zigzagging across that Mongolian grassland waste with its thorns and gusting wind. The only surprise came about two miles into the loop, where suddenly there was a steep plunge down into a hidden fold in the land, a sharp crevasse formed by the emergence of an underground stream running over mossy stones and flanked by thick bushes, even small trees as it went deeper. For this section of the course the runners would dip down and be hidden from all except each other and the marker at the far end of the fold, before the track climbed sharply up a gravelly incline back to the plain and the wind.

First time round I was flying. Of course, so was everyone else. With so few climbs the pace was fierce, set by a small, bored-looking kid with mechanically-whirling feet that never seemed to miss a beat. There'd be no comebacks today against this sort of talent: my best chance was to stay as close to that kid as possible and rely on my longer legs in a sprint at the finish.

Emotion drove me on: or was it the scorching absence of emotion? Maybe I *was* still the same Julian, but tougher, purer. Maybe I had become the Schwarzenegger metal skeleton. If so, I was glad. Whatever, I did manage to stay up in the top five as they, we, gradually pulled a little clear of the rest. Like I said, the pain grew fast to a level that I hadn't known existed: bursting heart, trembling, straining leg muscles, blurred, sweat-sore eyes. But I was flying with the others, and when we dipped surprisingly down into the hidden crevasse and my ankle—the same one as before—half-turned on the loose material, I barely felt it.

The abrupt quiet in that fold after the buffeting and sense of space above was unbelievable. We were completely alone in space and time. Just dull repeated footfalls and rasping breath from the five of us and sudden gushing sweat from the warmer more humid air. The killing climb out, forcing heavy limbs up to the fresh air again, was like surfacing when you've held your breath too long underwater.

The sweat didn't stop, though. My eyes were stinging with it, and now we were out my vest was blown cold and wet and heavy against my ribs, making it that much harder for my straining diaphragm to pull air down into oxygen-starved lungs. The mile or so back to the start to complete the first loop was a long dog-leg, no more surprises in terrain. By the end of it, I was pretty sure that I was coming down with something. A fever, probably.

I found, coming back past the faces of the watchers,

that I was trembling. Scalding and icy waves had started to surge through me.

Then, already, we had peeled off the home section into the second loop. *Why didn't I stop back there?* I wondered, fuzzily. *Why didn't I stop and tell Hewlett I was ill and just go home to sleep?* Still we five front-runners stayed in our pack a bit clear of the rest, but it seemed impossible that it was really *my* feet pummelling away under me, keeping me up there with the others.

At some point, the light had taken on a sickly yellow quality, dully picking out those few stunted thorn trees, killing sound.

We came again to the hidden gash in the land, and dipped suddenly down into the air that seemed warm and musty after the biting wind above. A comfortable place to lie and rest, on the moss next to the stream with my fingers in the cool water. Ahead of me, one of the five lost his footing at the base of the scree and we four streamed past, leaving him a few precious seconds behind.

The first three of us to finish would be up for a place in the national event. Which meant nothing to me except more hassle, more crap from Hewlett or his equivalent in whatever dump I got sent to, more pounding round a training lap for endless grey afternoons until my body was sick with it.

But then there wasn't anywhere else I would choose to be right now: nothing to be preferred to this pain and effort. Already the waves of all the *rest*, the whole rotten, stinking failure of my existence, were lapping at me, waiting to swamp me as I crossed the finish line. At least here, doing this, the white heat in this Terminator skeleton of my body could keep me free of the other for a while.

For the first time in two months, my brain switched abruptly into heavenly neutral, and I forgot all about lying down, hit the climb out of the gash hard, and became as automatic and merciless as the bored leader.

Eight or so wonderful minutes. Enough for any lifetime.

All the others were blown away except the one. Calm in knowing what I could do, I wound him gradually in, matched him stride for stride, neck-and-neck, bloody *bathed* in the puzzled, irritated look he shot across at me, and blasted across the finish at unstoppable, scorching pace.

And then surrendered to those inevitable waves.

A man I had never seen before found me and handed me my tracksuit.

'Er . . . you must be Julian. Jolly well done in the race! Amazing stuff! Um . . . I'm afraid Guy—Mr Hewlett— has gone. His wife, you know. They're not hopeful back at the hospital. I'm sure you know all about it: strictly speaking he shouldn't be at work at all. Anyway, he got a call and they suggested he should go back right away. So he asked me to give you a lift home later, with my lot.'

Then, seeing my blank look: 'That's our mini-bus over there. The green one. St Hugh's.'

I couldn't properly take it in. Something about Hewlett's wife. I was still half-dead from the race: still trying, too late, to dodge the moment when all the problems and disasters waiting at home would bulldoze into my conscious mind again, as well as my heart.

But . . . BUT . . . the synapses, the mental switches, opened and closed. Suddenly this stranger made some sort of sense, and I saw a *way*, a possibility, a chance. Instinct won over consciousness.

Sounding very calm, every inch the practised liar, I smiled and said, 'That's very kind, but you needn't worry.

I met some friends of my family over there. They offered to take me back. They only live in the next street.'

A doddle.

'All right. Fine then,' he said. 'And well done again for winning.'

He'd already forgotten me.

Completing the lie, covering loose ends, I went to get my medal and confirmation-of-entry form from the officials. 'I can't stay for the ceremony,' I told them blandly. 'My dad's ill: I have to get home.'

'Poor boy. Here you are. Off you go, then. Well done. Very well done.'

Then just one more thing. The most difficult, but it had to be done. I dived into the crowd and looked round at the possibilities. There was one kind-looking man standing alone: a pensioner, probably, maybe come to watch a grandson or something.

'Excuse me,' I said, 'I'm sorry to ask you, but do you have a phone I could use for a very quick call? My dad's ill and I want to get some news.'

He looked me up and down and said, 'You're the one that won the Junior just now, aren't you? Great piece of running, that. Don't know how you managed it, that finish.' Then, feeling in his jacket and pulling out a mobile: 'Here, go ahead.'

With the faintest of pangs of guilt, I dialled Liz's number. It rang and rang, but no answer and, for this once, no answer machine either. The man stood watching me while I pushed the 'hang-up' button and racked my brains for other possibilities. I couldn't remember Mrs Sykes's number, but thought I knew the school one. (I'd called it enough times now, pretending to be Dad.)

'Hello. I'd like to speak to Hayley Sykes, please. Yes, this is her . . . uncle. [She didn't have a father.] I've got some very serious family news for her. I wonder if she could be found?'

Amazingly it worked.

I waited for Hayley to be found while the pensioner watched me, doubtful now about having trusted his mobile to a stranger. Especially a black stranger.

'Hello?' came Hayley's voice.

And then I did it. I bailed out. Cut the cord. Gave up. The ugly words came out and peace poured in.

The pensioner was angry by the end, when I handed the mobile back. 'What the *hell* was all that about? Look, the battery's almost flat, the time you've been on. And it certainly didn't sound like anything to do with your father being ill.'

I looked at him blankly and walked away. I was free, in an open landscape.

Free.

14

A girl on a horse.

She spoke to me.

'Oh . . . hello. Were you one of the runners from today? From those races, or whatever they were.'

'Yes.'

'Oh.' Silence. 'You're not staying here, are you? I mean, the others must have all gone hours ago. You must be freezing.'

It was true that the hidden fold in the land was not warm now. I was shivering, wrapped in the blood-coloured blanket I'd swiped from the Red Cross tent. Every part of me ached from earlier. Apart from that I was numbly happy.

The girl was outlined against the last light of day, her horse standing peacefully near the lip of the gash. She tried again: 'You'll freeze to death. Don't stay down there.'

Why didn't she leave me alone? I said, 'I could be a murderer or a rapist. You should be careful.'

She seemed to find that funny and giggled a moment. 'You don't *look* very dangerous. Anyway, you'd have to run pretty fast to catch Angel, if you wanted to murder me.'

'Angel? That's the name of your horse?'

'Yes. Really it's Starburst Angel. He's my point-to-pointer. The name's a bit mushy, I know, but I was only eleven when I got him.'

'He's nice.'

'Yes, he's a darling. Do you know about horses?'

'Not really.'

'Oh.'

I thought that that was it, end of conversation. The horse was restless now and moved out of sight for a moment. Maybe she'd finally taken in what I'd said about being a rapist. She wouldn't have lasted two minutes where I came from. I huddled deeper into the blanket and tried to get comfortable, which was impossible as all the ground was damp and icy and hard.

The horse reappeared, very dim now as the light failed.

'Look,' came the girl's voice, a bit doubtful. 'You can't stay there. You really will freeze. If you want, you can come and sleep in our barn. Plenty of warm straw. And I could make you some hot tea.'

I said, 'You live on a farm?'

'Of course.'

'I've never been in a farm.'

'Oh.' She giggled again. 'How funny!'

It was as if I was an alien, landing on her planet. Or the other way round.

'How far is it? The barn.'

'Not far. We'll be there in ten minutes, riding.'

I pointed out the problems. 'I don't know how to ride. And I haven't got any horse.'

'Angel can take both of us, silly.'

'Flaming hell. You'll kill him.'

She giggled again. She was mad. 'You really *don't* know horses, do you? Anyway, you can jog behind if you prefer, since you're a runner. I'm going now, so it's up to you.'

It wasn't hard to decide, actually.

Somehow I got up onto the thing behind her and we bumped across the dark fields. The girl and the horse both had the same smell. Her hair tickled my face. Several times I almost fell off: it was a lot further off the ground than I'd imagined and there was nothing to hold on to except the girl, which didn't seem a good idea.

I thought of something. 'Don't you have a saddle?'

Her voice came back. 'Yes, but I sometimes ride like this to get a better technique. You can feel the way he moves . . . and sort of learn to move with it, I suppose. Makes you stronger too. Gripping with your thighs and keeping your posture. It's easy, with a saddle, after this.'

Starburst Angel was thawing out my bum nicely. The rest of me shivered.

I asked, 'Do you give lifts to lots of strangers?'

She said, 'No, this is the first time. Do you often sleep in the middle of nowhere in the middle of winter, in a tracksuit?'

'No, first time too,' I said. 'You're sharp.'

'Thanks.' She giggled.

The moon showed its first tiny edge over the horizon and I saw buildings looming up ahead.

The girl's name was Jill. She lived on a farm with her grandparents. Her parents were also farmers, fifty miles away, but: 'Dad and I don't really get on. And he and Mum are always fighting. And I wasn't allowed to ride much there. There was too much work to do.'

Here, she said, she *was* allowed. She had two ponies, besides Starburst Angel, and gave riding lessons to a few local kids. She also helped her grandparents. She got up at five-thirty every morning—five-flaming-thirty!—to get her morning chores done and still give time for the lessons and doing whatever it was that you had to do to look after horses, plus practising—training—on Starburst Angel.

It really was a different planet. But I was spinning free, now, so why not? Why not sleep in this girl's barn?

'What about school?' I asked.

'Oh, I left in June, when I turned sixteen. I did my GCSEs, but that kind of thing doesn't help much, with what I want.'

She told me all this while she got me sorted out, in the barn. Under the single wan bulb there she turned out to have lots of thick brown hair, brown eyes, and a tatty old green anorak, torn and covered with mud and horse hair. She wasn't exactly fat, but she certainly wasn't thin either.

'What about your grandparents?' I asked. 'Won't they mind me being here?'

'No. Don't try to sneak into the house to mug us all and steal the silver, though. We've got a big fierce dog.'

I couldn't tell if she was serious.

'There you are, then. There's a couple of Angel's old rugs. I'll come out again later with some tea and something to eat.'

'Thanks.'

'But tomorrow, as payment, I get to hear why you were going to sleep out there in the cold,' she said.

Maybe.

She was a liar. The big fierce dog was one of those black-and-white sheepdogs, not very large and as soft as butter. It woke me with its snuffling, pushing wet nose in the morning. It was completely dark and I had never been so cold, though whether it was the winter or the abyss of what I had done, I couldn't say. I groaned softly and tried to hide from the dog.

Jill's voice said brightly, 'Tea up.'

Spinning free, I reminded myself. No need even to look into the abyss. No need to acknowledge its existence. Be kind to yourself, Liz had said.

'What time is it?' I croaked.

'Half past six. You're lucky, I've let you lie in.'

'Oh, Christ. You're crazy.'

'Grandad says you can give us a morning's work for sleeping in the barn. If you want breakfast first, you'd better come in the next five minutes. Just knock on the green door—that's the kitchen—and come in.'

A morning's work! Ha flaming ha! I could hardly move. My body had seized up, like legs on old racehorses sometimes did, so they said on the box. From the pounding they got, like mine. Anyway, they couldn't make me work, if I didn't want.

When I went into the kitchen through the green door, Jill's grandad, sitting at a large square wooden table with a mountain of food on a plate in front of him, said, 'Saints preserve us, it's a darkie! You didn't tell us, Jill. Come on in then, lad, sit down, tell Minnie what you want.'

I said stonily to Jill, 'I think I'd better go,' but Minnie—Jill's tiny grandmother, standing with a huge spitting frying pan—said, 'Oh, don't mind him! Daft old fool fancies himself as some sort of Alf Garnett. Here, dear, what can I get you? Go if you want, but have something hot first, eh?'

Spinning free. I stood, not knowing what I was going to do for a moment, and then sat down at the table, next to Jill. The warm fug of the kitchen and the smell of hot food was too much to resist, after the freezing barn.

I was given my own massive plateful of eggs, fried bread, tomatoes, and beans. And another pint mug of dark brown tea. The daft old fool, Grandad, put five spoons of sugar in his mug and said cheerfully, 'No offence, lad. *I* don't care what the colour of a man's skin is. Not after being in the war.'

I couldn't decide about him and didn't know what he meant about the war, so kept quiet.

Next to me, Jill said, with her mouth full, 'You can help me with the loose boxes, this morning. Mucking out and sweeping the yard. And there's tack to clean for Saturday.'

Grandad chimed in: 'And the tractor shed wants a good sort out.'

They were quite clearly all mad. Shovelling away their stacks of fried food, swilling the gallons of tea, all looking bright and alive before seven o'clock on a dark winter's morning. At the stove, the tiny grandmother nodded and smiled and said, 'That's right, dear, eat up,' and came over with the great iron pan, trying to fit more on my plate.

I really was starving. If I decided to stay for the morning, I thought I might as well eat properly. Who could say where the next meal would come from?

The warm steamy kitchen felt very comfortable.

Even better, nobody asked why I had suddenly appeared. Or where I should be.

Nowhere, I thought. *There's nowhere I should be. I am free. Be kind.*

All the morning I slaved away. By the time it got properly light I was already hot enough to have taken off my tracksuit jacket, and the aches left by the race had been blasted away by the work.

Jill took Angel and the shaggy white ponies out of their boxes and with a vicious and bent two-pronged fork I removed all the pony shit and the old straw in swaying wheelbarrow loads to be dumped on a very large pile of even older shit and straw behind the barn; and then carried in new bales, which Jill cut open with an old kitchen knife, so that we could spread it out over the concrete.

Soon I had blisters from the pitchfork, but the old grandad appeared and took me off to the tractor shed, which was too full of broken old crap, bits of machines, and plastic fertilizer bags and stuff, to get the tractor properly in.

'There you are, lad! Clear that lot up for me, then have a good sweep out, eh, and you will have done me a big favour.'

Pitchforks, brooms, spades. Lucky I didn't play the piano or anything. My hands didn't have much skin left on them by lunchtime.

Jill laughed at me. 'You look the real farm boy now. Straw in your hair and everything. Except for that tracksuit.'

My tracksuit had pony shit on it. What did she want?

'Come on. Let's have lunch. Then you can help me with the tack.'

I said, 'Er, I don't know if . . . '

But she was going through the green door, calling back 'Come on!' and then I was going in too, and it was like breakfast all over again, with the grandmother, Minnie, nodding and smiling and banging out mountains of food and pints of tea, with the radio on, loud and un-listened-to, in the background. After the morning, I flaming needed that food. Then I thought I owed them a bit more work, for the meal, so I sat on a bale of straw in the barn and cleaned bridles and saddles with Jill. Scrubbing the leather clean of sweat and hair and mud and whatever else the horses managed to get into it, then oiling it all up and polishing . . .

Jill's hands were hard and red and like iron. Mine were covered with plasters.

After tack cleaning, there was grooming—brushing the animals—and then sweeping the yard while Jill was out exercising Angel. So much sweeping. What did they do when they didn't have a trained monkey?

By the time I got led through the green door again— all plans to move on today forgotten for the moment in my hunger—and had put away another of those elephant meals, I was so knackered I could barely keep my eyes open.

There was no need to make myself not think about the abyss: I couldn't think about anything.

Grandad said he was going to the pub. Jill said, 'We'll come too.'

The grandmother nodded and smiled over her pans. Christ! I thought.

But there was no escape from the energy of these mad people and soon I was sitting in the tiny village local, where there were about five people plus us, in my shit-stained tracksuit, sipping a half of lager, and felt too tired to care about looking a pillock.

Jill had changed into clean jeans and a thick, bright home-knitted jersey. She seemed as awake and alive as ever.

I smiled at her vaguely through the haze of beer and sleepiness.

'Poor Julian,' she teased. 'Poor city boy.'

15

The next day some jeans and an older version of Jill's jersey had been found for me, plus green wellies and thick, brown patched-up socks. By the second night I was sleeping in a tiny, ancient caravan that was parked up permanently behind the main house.

My plan to move on further from home had blown away, unnoticed, in the biting winter wind. So much for the new man-of-action Julian Egg.

Anyway, there was no *shortage* of action. From Jill banging in to the caravan with tea and a blast of cold air halfway through the night, and the stumbling, painful emergence out of my temporary home and across the yard to the haven of the green door, right up to my bemused and unsteady path back there at night to wriggle under the hairy, horsey blankets and remember nothing until it all began again . . . it was non-stop sweat and flaming effort.

It almost did for me and it felt marvellous.

The purpose of it, the routine, the physical hardness
. . . I'd never felt safer or more alive. Better and harder
than the toughest race, with not the smallest corner left in
the day to think about the unthinkable.

Jill poked me in the ribs and said, 'Well, Mr Mystery
Man, there's been nothing on TV or the radio about you,
so I suppose you're OK. Not a rapist or a murderer after
all.'

'No, nothing like that.' I couldn't understand why there
hadn't been something, some kind of publicity—they
must be looking for me, if only to stick me into so-called
'care'. But maybe it would just take longer: or maybe those
sorts of things didn't make it on to the radio, unless they
thought you'd been kidnapped or something. For the
moment Jill only teased and tried to fool me into giving
stuff away while we sat and scrubbed tack, or pummelled
away with the horse brushes, raising clouds of fine horsey
dust from the silky (Angel) or shaggy (the ponies) coats.

Things like: 'Have you started driving yet?' and 'Your
brother's older than you, right?'

She was not stupid, but much too . . . I don't know,
honest? open? simple? . . . to really fool anybody. 'I'll tell
you, soon . . . maybe,' I said. I didn't even get angry or
up-tight at her asking. The hard work, the endless cycle of
mucking out and sweeping and grooming and polishing,
and helping Grandad mend his fences, melted away my
tension. I wasn't like a coiled spring any more, even if I
didn't really plan to tell Jill anything.

Minnie asked no questions at all, seemed to have no
curiosity about why I'd suddenly dropped into their lives
out of nowhere. Grandad was more careful. 'Your business
is your own, son,' he said, suddenly looking sharply at
me, as I held a post straight ready for his (always perfect)
sledgehammer blow, 'so I won't ask anything you don't
want to tell. Except that I need your assurance that you're

142

sixteen or more and that you're not in trouble with the law. If you can satisfy me on that, then you're welcome to stay as long as you want. Heaven knows, the lass could certainly do with some help and a bit o' company.'

This old farmer, from the same mould as Jill herself, was no match for my ability to lie. It was such second nature to me that I'd given him the calm, direct promises that he asked for, before really considering it. Full eye contact and everything.

He clapped me on the shoulder and said, 'Well, that's all right, then. I'm happy to take your word, son.'

The trouble was, this time I felt shitty about it. And worse, it put an idea into my head, a tiny germ of an idea, anyway, which was something like: *You have brought your problems with you. You have not escaped after all.*

Or maybe that seed had already been there, rooted firmly in the dark inside my millions of microscopic synapse-switches.

On Friday and over the weekend, cars rolled up with squealing kids piling out before the wheels had stopped turning: mostly girls, all done up in expensive riding clothes—jodhpurs and boots and everything—and pigtails, running to give sugar and apples to their favourite pony. Hour after hour of them, some staying in the field to get walked round on a leading rope or schooled over fallen telegraph poles and stuff, some of them following Jill on Angel, out over the Mongolian land where I had raced.

Jill, zipped up in her falling-apart green anorak and with clouds of thick hair blowing round her head, was so *patient*. She never flipped at these kids, just encouraged them—'Knees in, that's it . . . heels pressed down . . . turn your toes in, sit up straight . . . well done! That's beautiful:

you look like part of the pony now, like you're *supposed* to be there. No, don't jerk at his mouth, he won't like that, keep those hands nice and relaxed. That's it.'—in an endless stream of smiling and nodding that old Minnie herself would be proud of.

I cleaned the animals out and learned how to 'tack' them up so that I could lead them, ready saddled, into the yard at the right times, or take them back at the end while Jill got paid and was polite and reassuring to the parents.

I could imagine the twins being the little riders, arriving with Dad maybe, dressed deliberately differently from anybody else and especially from each other. In shorts or macs or something. The Karkos would be forgotten in the dust under their beds. But that way lay madness . . .

Grandad, passing through the yard with his toolbox, said, 'All right, lad? You look a bit queer.'

'Yes. Fine. It's cool.' He'd already gone anyway.

A couple of times, back in the dark yard after the pub, Jill and I found that we were up close, with our arms around each other. A goodnight hug, that's all. She smelled of horse and soap and the rough wool of her jersey and her body was rounded and fit, supple from all the work and the riding. I could imagine her mouth against mine; sweet, teasing. She wouldn't take anything seriously. She giggled when I tried to be serious.

'Relax!' she said.

I was free, I told myself urgently. Free to enjoy this. Free to be kind to myself.

But it wasn't enough: the work and the food and the exhaustion and Jill's laughter and warmth against me. I felt like a new person, blessed by all the gods, born into a new universe. I was cleansed and released and happy.

And then that tiny speck of *before* that was left buried deep in me turned out not to be a tiny speck, but just a compacted version of the old Julian Egg. For three days, maybe, I pretended that I couldn't feel it, growing in me. Black and solid and shining like the Fuzzballs factory.

Or a black sea, maybe: heavy black liquid guilt, pulling at me with its current.

By the end of the weekend—five days since the trials—I knew that it hadn't worked. I'd pulled the elastic out as far as it would go, and now it was going to accelerate me *in* again, hurtling towards the things I couldn't face.

NO! I thought. *I am free now. The shapes are mine to make. There are no limits.*

And the answer came back, clear and cold and logical and certain: *You are doing what Dad did. Running away. Not coping. You are no better than him.*

The thought wrenched at my heart, stole away the joy of Jill and this new existence.

Sunday night Grandad wanted to watch football on the box, so Jill and I went alone to the pub. 'Tell me now, Mystery Man?' she said, maybe sensing what was happening inside me. Simple-smart Jill.

And I did.

She held my hand and I told her. And later we walked out on to the windswept plain, under a bright half moon, unspeaking. No need for words. In front of the caravan we hugged for the last time: I'd made my choice.

Madness. *Not* to choose this life, this girl. Bloody madness.

Monday morning I had the usual plateful from Minnie's iron pan, and then, with a terrible, sick-making tightness inside, hitched to the village to phone Liz. I had told Hayley to get Liz to handle whatever was done: to protect the twins as well as she could.

On the third ring Liz's voice said sharply, 'Hello. Yes?'

'Hello, Liz.'

A small silence. Then she said, surprisingly, 'You are *so* lucky!'

She sounded tired and pissed off, which wasn't so surprising maybe. Not the calm, tea-sipping guru with all the answers. Some perverse thing in me was pleased.

I said, 'Er . . . lucky?'

'Yes. Hayley said you would make contact. She was sure. She said you loved the twins too much. She said you wouldn't be able to see it through, your disappearance. So . . . I gave you until this morning. You've called in the nick of time. Lucky.'

The old nausea rose up and choked me.

'What do you mean?' The world was whirling. Such a crushing weight of feelings, hope and fear and hope again, that I could hardly breathe. Was I going to be back where I started? Had nothing changed?

Liz was not in a mood to care. Not about me. She said, 'Now listen very carefully, young man, because you have just one chance here. Several people have taken very large risks for you. *I* am one of those people: you *owe* me. So pull yourself together and *listen*!'

I thought of her saying *'Be kind to yourself'* before, when she had been my psychologist, and abruptly wanted to giggle. Maybe I'd caught Jill-itis. I was light headed. With an effort, I pulled myself together and listened.

Whether it was my time in the military routine of Jill's farm, or maybe Liz's brisk, don't-mess-me-around mood and the way she laid the situation out, the things I had to do next seemed quite easy.

Back to the farm, where I borrowed some of Jill's riding money and stood quietly a moment with her in Angel's stall. Then out on the road, hitching again, to the nearest town. When I'd got some new jeans—the borrowed ones were already in a state—I bought a train ticket to Cardiff Central, which turned out to be only walking distance from the address Liz had made me memorize.

There was a dizzy moment of panic again, standing outside the vaguely-familiar, red-brick terraced house with its gloomy net curtains and untidy little square of front garden; but only a split second. I rang the bell and chose a future. The best one available unless I wanted to leave my sisters alone forever.

Two hours later I was back on a train, a different line though, and going home. Feeling like people must feel after a long, long illness or something, when they make it outside for the first time. Weak and drained and feeble, like an old man, so that my hands shook with it. But also hopeful.

Hope was something new.

Back at home, I went straight to the Sykeses' place. Another day was dying. The twins, sparkling like new pins, were deep in Mrs Sykes's flowery armchairs, with plates of brownies balanced on their knees and milk rings round their mouths.

They tumbled over me in a torrent of limbs and kisses and nonsense.

Liz was there, watching me carefully like a hawk, unsmiling; and Mrs Sykes was fussing and getting more brownies and wiping away embarrassing tears.

And Hayley was there. Thin and white and strained and pretty. Very small and vulnerable. Very tough. I thought of what she'd done for me and my eyes met hers in a silent *thankyou* through all the fuss. I could see the same thing in her face that had made me feel . . . what? . . . threatened? . . . before. Now I just saw it neutrally.

Something to think about later.

16

Liz didn't give me her blessing to go to London. I went anyway.

She said, 'You're running away again! All this emotion: you hate it, don't you?'

'No,' I said stubbornly. 'You're wrong. Completely flaming wrong.'

'It's too soon. You've only just got back. We had a deal. I told you what the score was, Julian.'

I said, '*You* gave me the article.'

'Yes,' she admitted, tightly, 'but not so that you could go charging off, getting into more trouble.'

'You still don't believe Ferrin is doing anything wrong, do you? You still think I'm a nutcase.'

I couldn't get her to see why I had to go, so just went.

'It's only one day,' I said. 'A few hours. I'll be back tonight.'

'Don't do this, Julian, please!'

I left. I'd kept to the flaming deal. It was not much

longer that she'd have to help us. On the coach down to London I re-read the article her chemist friend had sent along. He'd scrawled: *I can't be sure. There are so many mistakes with your molecule. But the overall shape looks like one of the new breed of so-called 'intelligent chemicals'. Very BIG BUSINESS, or at least they will be soon. Read the piece and you'll see.*

The article was circled in red biro and headed:

Substances that learn to fit us like gloves. Goodbye scratch-and-sniff!

It was hard to understand—the whole magazine was for people who didn't get out much, research scientists and that lot, I think—but basically it seemed there were these new man-made chemicals, a bit like human pheromones or something, that could actually sort of 'read' our individual body chemistry, especially the chemistry of the brain (all those little packets of emotion) and then adapt themselves to fit our needs. Or to become something that we couldn't do without.

One way the mag described this thing was like one of those car engine tuning machines where they plug everything in and analyse what's happening inside and then can alter bits and tinker about to make the engine run cleaner or perform better or whatever you want. Except in this case the engine in your head ended up relying on the chemical tuning machine. Without that outside help it would go wrong or at least not perform brilliantly.

Commercially, the article talked about whether variations of the stuff could be used in aftershave and perfume, possibly to up your sex appeal and all that, or pumped into air-conditioning systems in offices to keep employees balanced and happy. There could be a thousand applications, it said. The intelligent chemical could be pre-designed to achieve all kinds of effects in the brain. (Let's face it, the scientists just enjoyed having a new toy: they were never really bothered how it got used.) But at the moment they were still having problems. Tests had only partially worked: some had produced 'mood-swings'. Then there were the problems of addiction and what the body and mind did when the chemicals were no longer present. All the people in the article agreed that the addictive quality of the substance would have to be removed, before it could be used commercially.

In his temple of Fuzzball information, the clean room, Hermes had scribbled *Is this it, the tiny thing that keeps them hooked?* across the molecule picture.

I thought again about Mrs Tanner's veiny old hand putting the two Karkos together on the floor while she stripped the twins' beds and re-made them. I thought about my sisters' erratic behaviour: dozily watching rubbish on the TV or kicking and screaming and getting into trouble. I thought about those children dying in Japan. I thought about how dizzy and sick I'd felt in that film, and in the factory at Duntocher.

No people in that factory, except the controller in his overhead box, shut off from the production area.

Liz had read the article too and shrugged and said, 'So? This is all just research.' She never stopped being the psychologist. I think she believed that all the way along I'd been getting obsessed about Ferrin and Fuzzballs just to avoid thinking about my problems at home. Now she'd sorted out the other, bought me some time at school, pushed me into going to that little brick house in Cardiff, she didn't see why I should bother any more with Fuzzballs. Her responsibilities were due to end tomorrow.

Fuzzballs.

Fuzzball Futures.

At last the scale of Ferrin's nightmare was clear in my head. All those millions of kids drinking thirstily at his fountain, unable to help themselves. What was he going to do in the Dome? Build a bigger, more impressive fountain? Keep his little disciples hooked?

I had to know.

Julian Egg to the flaming rescue.

A day trip wouldn't hurt. I'd be back in time for our new life beginning tomorrow. Then Christmas in only a few days. Liz was crazy if she thought *I* was.

The skies over London looked heavy and blank: snow was supposed to be coming. The temperatures had dived again, since being at the farm. Under my jacket I was wearing the old jersey of Jill's, bright and rough and thick. Hayley had asked where it had come from. Maybe she'd seen the long brown hairs on it. That was something else to sort out in my mind; but today the jersey reassured me.

I crossed London by tube and then took the new line to the Dome site. I was almost alone on the train, and as I got out and saw the platform cameras, I wondered if I should have come a different way. But then, they had the same cameras on every tube platform. Ferrin was hardly going to have taken over the London Underground, was he?

The site was closed off by the black, winter Thames on one side and high, portable fencing on the other. No electricity this time, but the same uniformed guards with dogs. Inside the cordon, 'our people' swarmed about in white overalls and white hard hats, backing trucks up into a giant side entrance, unloading crates, studying clipboards, disappearing back inside after the various loads.

The Dome itself crouched massively, like something preparing to jump on its prey, gleaming elbows sticking way up into the dull winter white.

Squatting down behind a skip, about ten metres outside the fence, I took out a throwaway camera, bought for the purpose, and started taking pictures. It all looked harmless, of course, just another big building site except there didn't seem as much shouting and nobody drinking tea and smoking—maybe Ferrin didn't allow those things. But there *had* to be something there to back up what I believed, since reading that article.

After half an hour, I decided that the 'something' must be inside. Logical. That's where I had to be too. Well fine, *I* was totally up for it, like on the night Hermes's place had been broken into. I felt fit and agile. That jersey smelled faintly of Starburst Angel, with his beautiful great head and bunched muscles.

A string of vans and trucks were entering and leaving the site, at least one every five minutes, all of them white, all of them stopping to show their papers at the barrier. I considered the possibilities. What I needed was a bunch of them arriving together, in a line, so that at least one had to stop or slow right down, level with my big skip.

Time ticked past: my watch told me I had four hours until I needed to be back at the coach station. Four hours to get in and find *it*—whatever *it* was—and then get out and back across London. Getting out would have to be easy, if I got in. *Christ*, it was freezing. I wanted to stand up and flap around a bit, to get warm: but stayed crouching. After a while, I started to feel less up-for-it. One leg was going to sleep. After about an hour, to make a change, I got out the sandwiches I'd brought and started to eat, sitting on the cold ground with my back against the skip. Three bites into sandwich number two I heard the rumble of an approaching engine: *several* approaching

engines. They ground along past the skip, one, two, three
. . . The fourth one had slowed right down to wait for its
mates to clear the entrance. Swearing, I threw away the
rest of my lunch and got up, almost falling over again on
the leg that had lost its blood supply. Gritting my teeth, I
clambered quickly up onto the skip side. The truck was
inching forwards, almost past, about to accelerate forward
to the gate, where two of its fellows had already been let
in.

Standing, swaying on tiptoes, I reached up and found
I could *just* get my finger tips over the top of the truck's
box section. But whether I would be able to pull myself up
. . . ? Oh *shit*, a foot to go before the chance was lost. I
jumped out and upwards, and hung on, flat against the
smooth white wall. The bright, machine-tooled ninety
degree edge at the top of the box started cutting into my
finger joints.

But now the truck was clear of the skip. If I fell off I'd
be seen. Aching once more from the hours of sweeping
and scrubbing and dung-moving, I hauled painfully
upwards. The truck was swinging slowly to the right now,
to line up at the gate for the security men. The one in front
was through and clear. My chin came over the top of the
box, and then my elbows. What if the driver looked in his
offside mirror, I wondered, and saw me there, clinging on
like a flaming mollusc.

The truck had stopped. The gate guard was on the other
side, looking at the driver's papers. Soon he would walk
slowly all around the vehicle, before raising the barrier.
That's what he did with each truck and van and even the
cars. He would look underneath too.

I heard the security man's voice: 'Wait there then,
mate, while I have a butcher's!' With a last painful heave,
I swung one leg up, got my foot over the rim, and then
rolled inwards to the centre of the white top, bringing the

trailing leg with me. Once there I lay spread-eagled and panting and hoping that the driver hadn't felt or heard the vibrations of my weight on the thin steel.

Thirty seconds later I was in. Not just inside the fence, but inside the Dome too. The truck had driven straight in. Then . . . *then* the problem with my idea became obvious. Outside I'd been invisible, flat against the top of that high truck. Inside was different. A giant mess of scaffolding had been put up on one side, as big as a roller-coaster park, and serviced by eight or ten cherry-pickers. In the middle of it all, Fuzzball Futures was growing. Massive shining and garish figures of some of the Fuzzball creatures were being built, with walkways connecting them and entrances down near the toes or claws or flippers or whatever they had. Near the foot, smaller buildings sprouted in the shape of jagged rocks or strange plants. Up above, at the pinnacle of the scaffolding towers, the translucent Dome skin was being transformed into a grey-pink-purple sky.

The whole lot was supposed to make you think of an alien landscape, I suppose.

I didn't get more than a few seconds to check it out, though, because of the thing I hadn't thought of. With that scaffolding stretching up well above where I was lying— a nice clear dark shape on a white surface—the guys working up there saw me easily and immediately.

There were shouts, whistles blew, running feet, and then a ladder poked over the truck top. A moment later a face appeared: one of the guards, a skinhead like an older, bigger, nastier version of Big Trev.

'All right then, you little ****, let's have you down off the ****ing truck. Now!'

I thought about lashing out with my foot. I could easily connect with his ****ing face and knock him off the ****ing ladder. But after that there wouldn't be much else to do—I'd never make the gate—so I did what he said and got down off the ****ing truck.

There were five security guys at the bottom, plus a growling, bare-teethed Rottweiler. They held me still with my arms painfully twisted up behind my back and searched me. The throwaway camera was found, in my sock, and thrown on the floor, disappearing under a large black boot with a snapping and popping of cheap plastic.

I suddenly thought that maybe I should be afraid. Liz's words—' . . . charging off, getting into trouble'—floated through my brain.

Another man was coming over. It didn't surprise me at all that he was compact, dark-haired, dark-eyed, dressed in an expensive, almost-black suit. Maybe there *was* only the one man, where I saw three. He looked at me briefly and said, 'Lock him in a Portakabin. Have someone watch him. The boss can decide about him, later.'

To me he said, 'Trespassing is a very serious thing, young man. I hope you'll think about that while you're cooling off.'

I think he said that to make it sound as if they weren't locking me up because of the molecule and whatever terrible thing they were planning to do at Fuzzball Futures, but just because I'd come in where I wasn't supposed to.

One of the security men took up the idea, as they marched me to a plain white Portakabin sitting by itself in the middle of the huge floorspace: 'Yeah, that's right,' he said gruffly. 'What if you got 'urt by a bit 've fallin' scaffold or somefing, eh? Then yer mum'd be bleedin' suin' us, wouldn't she?'

They must have thought I was crazy, to believe that rubbish.

I stayed silent. We reached the cabin and I was put in one of its tiny rooms, the door locked behind me. I heard feet disappearing, but also the scrape of a chair outside, so no doubt someone was watching the door as instructed.

I slumped down against the wall and thought: *Oh ****!*

Time passed and I got very cold. I did some exercises, squat thrusts and press-ups and leg stretches. I needed to keep my muscles warm for whatever chance came my way for escape.

Then, after a while, I just sat on the floor, waiting.

I tried to think about what I had seen, out there in the Dome. *Think! There must be something there, to need the security men and the dogs.* But whatever it was, I couldn't bring it into my mind.

Later—how much later? My watch didn't seem to be working: I must have banged it or something—a man brought me some tea. He left it next to me on the floor without a word. I picked up the scalding plastic cup and soaked up the heat. The hot sugary tea burned down my throat, making me shudder.

I couldn't think any more about evidence against Ferrin. Instead I thought about me being here and what they would do to me. The last coaches and trains home must have gone by now. Liz was right: I was a nutcase.

Then I really *did* think about that. Maybe she *was* right. Perhaps I was mad. Everyone else would be able to see it, see how I didn't fit in or do the right things or know how to behave normally; but I *wouldn't* be able to see it. The idea was terrifying.

How did you know if you were mad?

What was I doing here? I could be at home, or with Hayley, or in my little caravan, warm with beer and Jill's livewire energy. Maybe madness was . . . what did they call it? Congenital. Part of my family. Handed down by my loopy mother and my scared, no-good father.

All the things I'd done since Dad had left went spiralling helter-skelter through my head. A twisted, painful mess. I saw those things differently now. Oh, Christ, I *was* mad. No flaming doubt about it. All that money lost and Hayley lost too and the twins having to just . . . survive. All those lies at school and to Mrs Tanner and Hayley's mum. Hating and cursing Hewlett without knowing that his wife was ill, close to death maybe. Never seeing with other eyes. Everything messed up in only two or three months. And all the time, my worrying on and on about Fuzzballs.

I should be locked up.

I was.

Gradually, miserably, I slipped into sleep, still propped against the wall.

From time to time I woke, wretched, freezing cold, sweating, hopeless. Always in darkness: the light was off and I couldn't get up to turn it on.

I was delirious. Maybe there'd been something in that tea. *I have been kidnapped,* I thought. *I am in the Millennium Dome. I have been drugged. Fooled like a defenceless baby.*

Then I remembered again that I'd lost the plot. All that stuff about Ferrin and intelligent chemicals, it was just flaming crap. Forget the psy-*chia*-trist: call for the white van.

At some point I think more tea came, though I'm not sure. Then there was more sleep, and this time . . . dreams.

I dreamt that I was in an operating theatre, under the knife at this very moment. I could feel the icy, precise incision down the front of my ribcage. I had collapsed in the race, the Area Trials, and now they were going to look at my heart. Anything else since then was just hallucination from the anaesthetic.

'Parts of this heart have hardened,' explained the surgeon to onlooking students, 'so that those parts do not now move freely and flexibly. The strain this creates is tremendous. Other parts have been made to work too hard: they are weakened and unreliable.'

I heard Sophie say, 'Can *we* touch?' and the surgeon said, 'I do not see what harm you could do, child. Just a little squeeze then.'

The pain was huge.

In another, I was knocked, bruised, cut. Layer upon layer of dusty, dry skin was removed and fell around my feet. When I squinted out through eyes that were heavy and awkward, a chisel and hammer loomed, held gently, lovingly by white hands that had even whiter Victorian lace cuffs half covering them.

'I cannot choose your shape, my darling. It is there already for me to find.'

Countless others, swimming through me like shoals of fish.

Julian.

Jules.

Occasionally one of the fish spoke to me, touched me, brushed gently against the hardened and the strained parts of the heart.

You are not alone. I love you. And it's not just me, Jules . . .

I jerked fully awake. I was lying face down on the dusty floor and colder than a human being could be. Whether it was day or night was impossible to tell. I could have been in this room for a day or more. I was hungry and parched and dizzy and sick. And somewhere in my mess of emotion and thought-carrying chemicals, a neat little package arrived at the conscious part of my brain, saying, *If you want to try to fight back, you must do it now. Next time you wake you will be past it. Past caring.*

It was true. It didn't matter if I was mad or right about

Ferrin or about anything. The problem right now was beautifully precise and very clear. I directed my thoughts savagely at the world in general and thought *sod you!* . . . and rolled stiffly over onto my belly, forced my hands down against the cold, metallic floor and made my body rise. Then fall. Then—oh, flaming Christ!—rise again.

After ten press-ups I was dripping in sweat once more. My body must be reeking. The prison room reeked: they'd put in a bucket for a toilet. Ten more press-ups. Then some stretching, straightening out aching, knotted limbs.

Sod you! I thought with each twinge. *Sod you!* with each circle of my arms, each dip onto the floor, each high kick.

This could even be Christmas Day, I thought.

Next time the tea came I gulped it down while the security man watched me and then, when he'd gone, made myself sick, fingers touching the back of my throat so that I retched down my front and over the floor. I had never done that before and it was disgusting, horrible, degrading. *Sod you, Lucky Ferrin!* I thought, wiping my mouth with the back of my hand. If the tea was drugged, they would think I was asleep soon now. They would lower their guard.

Think, Julian Egg. Why are you here? How will you escape? What do your captors want?

Press up, squat thrust, run softly on the spot.

There was nothing in the cell, nothing that could be a weapon, nothing to open the door.

Think, Julian Egg.

Press up. Squat thrust. Leg stretches. Jumping jacks.

Then noises, someone coming. I slumped lifeless and sickly against the wall.

Julian. Jules. I love you.

Someone came in. They were bending over me. Taking the cup? Checking I was asleep? No, it was a blanket:

159

someone was putting a rough blanket or something over me. As they pulled it up under my chin, I exploded upwards, grabbing hold of the guy's shoulders, wrestling him sideways back down to the floor as I rose up, and then bundling him up in his own blanket.

It was done in five seconds. In six I was out of the Portakabin and blinking in the bright lights of the Dome building site. Instinct told me that it was night, but the place still seemed full of people; all the white-uniformed workers going on with nursing Fuzzball Futures into life. The guy behind in the cabin was banging away at the door I'd locked after me and calling to his mates. Already I'd been seen: there were the whistles again and the shouts. The whole thing was useless before it even got started.

Just flaming do it, Julian Egg, you loser.

I put my head down and ran, trainers kissing the concrete like falling rain, seeing faces looming up in front of me, hands grabbing . . . I struck out hard, not slowing at all. One man stepped into my path and got hold of my shoulders, and I twisted sideways and forwards, dropping all the weight down over one knee, so that he fell heavily backwards, off balance and flailing with his empty hands. As I passed the new towering Fuzzball shapes, half-completed and showing bare wiring and soon-to-be concealed lighting systems, I caught a glimpse of thin metallic tubing, twisting up into the innards of the creatures. It was like the tubing you get for gas fires and stoves, and even while I was barging another guy with my shoulder, I thought: *That's it! That's where the molecule will be hidden*.

Sprinting through the gaping entrance they used for the trucks—out into a surprising night full of swirling snowflakes—I heard the dogs barking excitedly. Fifty metres to go to the gate. Two security men were on my heels, another one moving to stand in front of the barrier. I didn't have a clue where the dogs were.

With a wild surge of adrenalin through my straining heart, I upped the pace a notch and moved away from the two pursuers, hearing their gasping and swearing. Then, as I reached the one in front—the last one!—I suddenly changed direction; feinting first to his right and then flicking back lightly to his left, leaving him, too, off balance, so that I was able to push him down into the snow.

Freedom!

A last figure I hadn't seen moved in quickly from the right. I had a split second view of one of those savage dogs, all teeth and bristling fur, straining on its chain . . .

But the man didn't slip the leash and I was out. Skidding sideways and banging into a parked car as my feet failed to grip, then off towards the lights hanging in the sky over central London, running fast and easily through the dancing whiteness, pulling in litres and litres of beautiful, filthy London air.

F**k, the night was *cold*. Even if I hadn't needed the distance from my kidnappers, I would have had to run to stop from freezing to death. Parked cars were glazed with frost. The river, when I came back to it further west, was hung over with icy mist. No one stirred. Maybe Ferrin had drugged the whole city. Anything was possible in the life that my life had become.

On. And on. Not bothering with trying to find transport—probably nothing was running at this time anyway, whatever time it was—the first goosepimples long since replaced by chilling sweat, another layer of grime to soak into my T-shirt and Jill's jersey.

An hour? Two? It seemed forever.

Finally the motor started to wind down, out of fuel, out of energy, out of effort. God knew where I was. I'd cut backwards and forwards across the city, always heading towards the lighter, busier part, the part that never slept, making it as difficult as I could for any of those men in white to find me. At some point I'd crossed the river. Lambeth Bridge, I thought it was, maybe. Now, as I finally slowed down to a walk and started to shiver once again, I seemed to be in some posh area. Great square white stone houses, little parks between them, wide pavements, Mercs and Lotuses and huge Alfa Romeos parked along the streets.

Coming round another corner, starting to stumble now with exhaustion, I found I was in another little square, large houses round the outside and an area of grass and bushes enclosed by low iron railings in the centre.

The streetlights hadn't turned off yet and their orangey glow competed with the new paler light from above as another day struggled to dawn.

I vaulted the railings.

And saw that the tiny park, carpeted in crisp, pure white, was hosting a display of four or five pieces of sculpture, set here and there in no kind of ordered way, with a little board pegged into the grass beside each.

Perhaps I had guided my chemical streams and packets unhesitatingly to this moment. System number one million and one. Choose a bet with odds too large to imagine and offer your soul. Swim free in the seas of chance.

I walked towards the central piece of sculpture and knew the work. Knew the way the form had been drawn out. Had seen the artist do it many times.

The board read:

ANGELIC SELF

One of a series of pieces from acclaimed local sculptor, Claire Egg.
Completed April, 1999.   Material: oolitic limestone

I had forgotten how beautiful she was. The piece had been made for this moment. A reaching, graceful, balanced figure, every atom focused upwards, flying towards the skies as they emptied ever-larger flakes of pure white.

Do you know what peace is? Do you know what it is to be whole?

I found a spot under bushes. My hands made a hollow in the leafy earth and, when I was lying down, scooped more leaves over me, and then spread a layer of newspaper, found discarded on a bench.

Incredibly, I was warm at last.

Between waking and sleeping, that sentence came again into my head. Advice from my teasing, naïve, unhappy young mother. *We can but do the things we are given to do . . . with all our heart and mind and effort.*

With a great sleepy shudder I realized that that was what I had done. My best. In all things.

When I woke, I would be facing forwards, absolved of all responsibility. Moving into the new part of our lives.

Everything was clear now.

17

I let Ferrin go. Enough was enough.

The only thing I did was put all the things I'd learned, and everything I guessed, down on paper. From Hermes to the metal tubing at the Dome. Then I added a copy of the article on 'intelligent' chemicals, and sent the whole lot anonymously to the police.

I sent an identical package to Ferrin himself, c/o The Millennium Dome.

The last one got left with Liz, just in case.

'You fruitcake,' she said; but I told her, 'That's it. Nothing more after this. I promise.'

All that time, sweating and dreaming as a prisoner down in London, had been just one night. Perhaps when I broke free from the Dome it had actually only been late evening. Who knows. Liz rolled her eyes when I told her, and said that she'd known I was going to piss people off, charging down there like a madman.

I don't think she believed any of it, even then.

'No more nights away. No more nonsense,' she said.

'No. Promise.'

I wasn't interested any more anyway. I couldn't flaming care less, didn't know why I ever had.

I went round grinning like an idiot.

I took a long, scalding bath.

I phoned Hayley and spewed out happy nonsense at her.

The twins tumbled around the place, poking at things under the tree, giggling, hanging on Aunt June's sleeves.

Aunt June was not as I remembered her.

She was quiet and careful, rather faded and old, but kind.

'You silly boy!' she said. 'Trying to do everything yourself. You're just a child!'

I didn't tell her anything about the Fuzzballs. When the twins had gone to bed, we sat together in the living room and watched *The Bill* and *Friends* and all that rubbish, with the Christmas lights reflecting faintly off the screen.

'You silly boy,' she murmured, over her clicking knitting needles.

27 January:

In a surprise, last-minute move, Fuzzball billionaire 'Lucky' Ferrin today issued a statement confirming yesterday's rumours that work on the new Dome theme park, Fuzzball Futures, is to be abandoned. Mr Ferrin is reported to have blamed 'uncertainty amongst investors' and 'unanswered questions concerning the future of sterling' for the pull-out.

He is now believed to be switching his attention to the markets of the Far East.

Some time later, in March maybe, I remembered the Spence that Hermes had given me, and wondered if I had been stupid. Perhaps I hadn't needed to go through all that . . . But when I looked in the stairs cupboard, there was no Spence.

No Hermes either. I never knew what happened to him. Maybe he'd gone home, to Greece, land of *kataifi*.

18

The thrumming was getting louder. Swelling, powerful, earth-shaking.

The sun was hot on our faces, a mini-May-heatwave. Aunt June mopped away with a red handkerchief, but Hayley stayed cool under a straw hat.

The twins jumped up and down. 'Here they come, here they come, here they come . . . oooohhhh!'

They lapsed into silence.

The six of us stood in wonder as the surging tide of horses, a starburst of muscle and bright silk and beauty of form, spilled over the green turf and past us in a heart-stopping flash.

'Quite something,' June said.

Hayley ran her fingertips over my ribs and looked up at me, glowing.

Liz, watching, said, 'Let's get an ice cream.'

'*Yeah! Yeah! Yeah! Nice cream!*' shouted Sophie and Tanya.

'Beep beep,' I said.

What else?

What else was a letter wedged deep under my mattress.
A letter to Mum, buried deep, deep from the world until
I'd decided.

Oh yes. You probably wanted to know about Last Chance.
(Remember him?)
True to his name, he came in last, apparently.
Well, you can't expect flaming miracles, can you?